"I Can't Marry
I Won't Be Your Wife!

His hands caught hers and he drew her relentlessly closer with his masculine strength. She tried to look away but could not; her whole body was tense with waiting and he knew it. If she were wise, she thought to herself, she would run away, have nothing more to do with him.

"So you don't want to be my wife? But you *do* want to kiss me, don't you?"

She could not deny it. "Yes," she whispered.

ELIZABETH HUNTER
uses the world as her backdrop. She paints with broad and colorful strokes, yet she is meticulous in her eye for detail. Well-known for her warm understanding of her delightful characters, she is internationally beloved by her loyal and enthusiastic readers.

Dear Reader:

Silhouette Romances is an exciting new publishing venture. We will be presenting the very finest writers of contemporary romantic fiction as well as outstanding new talent in this field. It is our hope that our stories, our heroes and our heroines will give you, the reader, all you want from romantic fiction.

Also, *you* play an important part in our future plans for Silhouette Romances. We welcome any suggestions or comments on our books and I invite you to write to us at the address below.

So, enjoy this book and all the wonderful romances from Silhouette. They're for *you!*

Karen Solem
Editor-in-Chief
Silhouette Books
P. O. Box 769
New York, N.Y. 10019

ELIZABETH HUNTER
The Lion's Shadow

Silhouette Romance

Published by Silhouette Books New York

SILHOUETTE BOOKS, a Simon & Schuster Division of
GULF & WESTERN CORPORATION
1230 Avenue of the Americas, New York, N.Y. 10020

SILHOUETTE BOOKS, a Simon & Schuster division of
GULF & WESTERN CORPORATION
1230 Avenue of the Americas, New York, N.Y. 10020

Distributed by Pocket Books

ISBN: 0-671-57018-8

First Silhouette printing July, 1980

10 9 8 7 6 5 4 3 2

The Lion's Shadow

Chapter One

The bus had been a long time coming. Gemma Savage eased the bag containing the exercise books she was taking home to correct on her shoulder and jumped lightly onto the platform at the back. To her relief she saw an empty seat halfway down and made toward it with the determination of one who has had a long, hard day. She was only just in time, for barely had she smoothed her skirts over her knees when she felt the full impact of a large male body landing on top of her. She gave an exasperated sound of annoyance, pushing him away from her, when the bus lurched forward for a second time and she found herself once more squashed flat beneath him.

The man steadied himself by thrusting both knees into her thigh with a bruising intensity. It was easy to see that he was unaccustomed to the rigors of rush hour travel and Gemma felt a fleeting sympathy for him, or she would have if he had only removed his kneecap from where it had come into contact with her hipbone. For some reason that she could not analyze the contact was acutely embarrassing to her. She tried to wriggle away from him, but the woman who shared the seat with her poked at her with her basket in response and Gemma desisted.

"Buona sera, bellissima signorina!"

It was said with a casual inclination of the head which Gemma could see out of the corner of her eye. She refused to look directly at him, but she already knew exactly what he looked like. She could not be unaware of the power that was packed into that wide-shouldered body, nor of the crisp, black hair and the flash of a pair of dark eyes that she knew full well had already looked her up and down with no detail of her appearance escaping them.

"Buona sera, signore," she answered politely.

His eyebrows rose. "You speak Italian, *signorina?*"

The last thing she had wanted was to get into a conversation with him. She gave him a haughty look, her green eyes, the shade of duckweed that grows on any village pond, not quite meeting his.

"Will you please stand on your own feet?" she suggested coldly.

"I would if I had somewhere to put them." He bent down and retrieved her bag from the floor. "Yours?" he asked her.

She snatched it from him, hugging it to her as if it were her most precious possession.

"What do you keep in it?" he inquired.

"That's nothing to do with you!"

His knees were no longer grinding into her flesh but she could still feel them against her thigh. It was ridiculous to be so self-conscious, she thought, just because a personable man was standing next to her on the bus. It was not an occasion to allow one's imagination to run riot, not that that had ever been her way in the past. She had sometimes wished she had had more of her sister's romantic dash instead of being her own prosaic self. Then she wished she had not thought about her sister for it was only today that she had begun to forget. The pain of her memories showed in her eyes and in the droop of the generous curves to her mouth. Her sister had been far too young to have had her life ended in such a cruel manner and, although the two of them had had little enough in common, Gemma missed her unbearably. It should have been her father whom she missed more, but he had withdrawn from life many years before, perhaps even when her mother had died giving birth to her younger child, Gemma herself. Even so, Gemma had always been told that she had more of her father in her than her vivacious Italian mother. Her sister Giulia had been the Italian one, up and down, either laughing or crying, and quite unconcerned with anything that did not immediately affect herself.

"Beautiful women should be used to people expressing an interest in them," the man said lightly.

Gemma was recalled to the present with a bang. She looked him full in the face, noting the distinguished planes to his face, the cruel smile that lingered at the corners of his mouth, and the enigmatic gaze which she felt instinctively saw more than most. What did it see in her? She put an agitated hand up to the heavy bun she wore at the nape of her neck and twisted it more firmly into position. Her hair was the color of golden syrup and should have been her pride and joy, but all her life she had longed to have the black hair of her sister and her dark, Italian looks. Even her skin refused to tan when she went out in the sun, though she was fortunate in that it didn't burn either, it was just that she was naturally pale and there was nothing she could do about it, any more than she could do anything about the strange greenish color her eyelids had, almost as if they were determined to reflect the green of her eyes without benefit of artifice.

"I am not beautiful," she stated with the firmness of one who knows she speaks the truth. "And this is where I get out," she added in relief.

She stood up, only then realizing that she still had to get past the stranger before she could push her way down the crowded aisle to the open platform at the back. She blinked nervously, disliking herself for her reaction to him almost as much as she was disliking him.

"Excuse me," she said.

"*Prego.*" Somehow he achieved the impossible and allowed her to slip past him, but he did not take her seat as she had expected, but followed her down the aisle, his fingers twisting in the strings of her bag to make sure that he kept in contact with her.

Gemma turned her head crossly. "Let go!" she snapped.

"I believe you are a schoolteacher," he returned, transferring his hold on her bag to her upper arm. "You have a certain way of giving orders that comes with much practice, only I am not a schoolboy, *signorina*, and I have a mind of my own."

How could she doubt it? Anyone less like a schoolboy it would be hard to imagine, but that did not excuse his actions from the moment he had first collided with her, and she had no intention of pandering to his pride by allowing him to see that his touch on her arm had scattered her wits to the four winds and had brought a funny lump into her throat that refused to go away.

"*Signore*," she began, "in England—"

He shrugged his shoulders. "I am sorry, *signorina*, but this happens to be my stop too."

She eyed him suspiciously. "Are you sure?"

He produced a piece of paper from his breast pocket. "See for yourself," he invited her.

She took the piece of paper from him and unfolded it. To her surprise she saw her own name neatly printed in an ornate, old-fashioned script that she had seen often before, and it was her address that followed it, as it had been written so frequently in the past on letters for her sister from their grandmother.

"You've come from *her!*" she gasped.

The bus lurched to a stop and she stepped down off the platform. A gust of wind, cold with the last of the winter, caught at her coat, revealing her long, shapely legs to his gaze.

"How do you know Nonna?" she demanded, bitterly aware of her rising color as he made no effort to disguise his appreciation of what the wind had revealed.

"I know her well," he said.

She was still standing in the same spot, one foot on.

the pavement and one in the gutter. He was frowning at her. "Are you disappointed that I'm the other grand-daughter?" she asked him.

"Is that how you think of yourself? As the 'other' granddaughter?"

It wasn't any of his business, of course, but that was exactly how she thought about herself. She had been the other one ever since she could remember. Her father had made no secret of his preference for her older sister saying that she reminded him of his beloved wife, and it had always been Giulia who had been sent to Venice to visit their grandmother. The excuse had always been that it had been too expensive to send them both, but Gemma had known from the very first moment when she had compared her own looks to those of her sister what the reason had really been— Giulia had belonged to both sides of the family and Gemma did not.

She nodded her head. "I'm a changeling," she explained. "I'm not like anyone else in the family."

His frown deepened. "A changeling? I am not sure I know what this word means? I understood it to mean an idiot, or a particularly fickle person?"

She opened her eyes wide. "Once upon a time it meant a child left by the fairies in exchange for a human baby."

"But don't you know—" He stopped. "Are we going to stand out here in the cold wind for much longer?" he asked instead.

The interest and admiration had gone. In its place was an impatience that she knew well. "You think I'm sorry for myself, don't you? But I'm not. Giulia was my best friend as well as being my sister. I was never jealous of her."

"You had no need to be," he said.

What did he know about it? she wondered. Who was he anyway? He seemed an unusual messenger for her very conventional grandmother to have sent, though she only had Giulia's word for what her grandmother was like because her grandmother never left Venice these days and Gemma had never visited her there.

"I suppose you are who you say you are?" she said aloud, chewing on her lower lip and frowning.

"I haven't yet said who I am," he reminded her sharply. "Please may we get out of this wind and I will answer any questions you like to put to me?"

She laughed at him. "Surely a man of your stamp is not worried by a little wind?" she scoffed. She felt better now that she had had her own back.

"I am not used to your English weather, nor your English notions of hospitality. Are you afraid to ask me to share a cup of tea with you?"

"Why should I be afraid?"

He shrugged. It was a very Italian gesture. "Girls who are used to being overlooked have more time in which to exercise their imaginations as to what might happen to them at the hands of a strange man," he said pointedly.

"*You* didn't overlook me," she pointed out. "You said I was beautiful. Very beautiful," she added smugly.

"An Italian will call most girls beautiful if he thinks it will please them. You make too much of too little, *signorina.*"

"An English girl learns at her mother's knee never to believe what an Italian says," she retorted. "You may come in if you must, *signore*, but I certainly have no intention of making you tea!"

He smiled kindly at her, amused. "Then I shall make the tea and you shall share it with me. Is this where you live?"

She looked at the shabby front door, remembering how her father had said it was time he gave it a lick of paint on that fateful day when both he and Giulia had been killed on the nearby motorway. Gemma was used to its shabbiness, but she wished the place looked a little less poverty-stricken now. A teacher didn't make a great deal in her first year and she had never imagined that it could be so expensive supporting herself and the house she had always known as home.

She took out her key and turned the lock, preceding him through the door. A letter in her grandmother's writing and bearing her strong, distinctive scent fluttered down from the letter-box to come to rest at her feet. She stooped to pick it up, but he was before her. He read the name and address on the envelope carefully before handing it to her.

"If you show me where the kitchen is, I will make the tea while you read your letter. I am the Marco Andreotti she refers to. I should have not thought a letter of introduction was necessary these days, but it seems the signora knows her granddaughter better than I do. She said it would put your mind at rest to know I could be trusted."

"Why should I have to trust you?" Gemma asked. "Why have you come?"

He put out a hand, pressing home one of the hairpins

she used to discipline her hair into the nape of her neck. She felt a *frisson* of something very like fear go down her spine and she jerked away from him, her eyes angry and very bright.

"I have come to take you to your grandmother," he said.

"To *take* me to her? I'm hardly a child to be taken anywhere! Besides I don't know Nonna. She was more Giulia's grandmother than she ever was mine. Why should she want to see me now?"

"How should I know? Perhaps she feels she has a duty to you, even if you feel none toward her."

Gemma's jaw dropped. "But—"

"You may not have bothered yourself to visit her before," the man went on grimly, "but now I am here to see that you do. Your mother was her only child and she is old and lonely. If it gives her any pleasure to see you, then see you she will!"

"She saw Giulia every year," Gemma pointed out.

"But never her younger granddaughter? Why not?"

"Because Giulia was the Italian one. Father couldn't afford to send us both—"

"And how often do you suppose he paid for your sister to go to Venice? You'll have to think of a better excuse than that. The Contessa is no fool even if she is old."

The title grated oddly on Gemma's ears. She could only remember her grandmother's rank being mentioned once before and that had been by Giulia after her first visit to Venice.

"Nonna's house is falling down," the little girl had told her father and sister, "but she likes it that way. *I* call her Nonna, but there's a horrid boy who lives in a tiny apartment at the poor end of the *calle,* and *he* calls her Donna Maria. In English that would be Lady Mary, wouldn't it? I expect it's because she's a Contessa."

"Much good it does her!" their father had retorted. "She probably invented the title for herself because she liked the sound of it." Mr. Savage had seldom had anything kind to say about his wife's family.

Giulia had shrugged bony shoulders. "I think she's a witch," she had said dreamily. Both Giulia and Gemma had been much interested in witches at the time. "Only she doesn't have one familiar, she has lots and lots. There are big, smelly cats in every room."

"Is she very old?" Gemma asked Marco Andreotti. She had always pictured her grandmother as having ill-kempt gray locks of hair protruding under the kind of hat she had once seen on a Welshwoman in national dress.

His face softened. "It depends what you mean by old. She is one of the best friends I have had in my life." His lips twisted into a wry smile. "Only the young and spoiled make no allowances for the demands of old age. Are you afraid you will be bored by her company?"

Gemma flushed. "I've never thought about it."

She kicked off her shoes and turned her back on her visitor, opening her grandmother's letter. The carpet was warm from the fire and she wriggled her toes in the pile, glad to be free of the plain walking shoes she wore for work.

"The stamps are pretty," she commented, uneasily aware of his disapproving silence. "If you're going to make tea," she added, not looking up, "the kitchen is through there." She waved her hand in the general direction of the door that led from the living room into the kitchen.

Marco Andreotti stood where he was, his arms folded across his chest surveying her, his eyes as hard and as cold as stones. Gemma tried to pay him no attention, concentrating with increasing desperation on the letter in her hands, but the beautiful, copper-plate letters swam into each other. Her hands began to shake, betraying her nervousness and firing her anger with this strange man who was proving impossible to ignore.

"You look a mess," he said at last. "Before you meet your grandmother you'd better tidy yourself up and mend your manners. She'd be ashamed to see you now."

"What makes you think I shall be seeing my grandmother?" Gemma shot back at him.

"What makes you think you will not?"

She lowered the thin, scented page she was reading. "It's the middle of the term, *signore*. My *first* term. I can't leave at a moment's notice just because my grandmother has chosen to remember that I exist! I have my career to consider."

"Career?" He was amused now. "The only career worthy of Donna Maria's granddaughter is the traditional one of marriage and bringing babies into the world."

Gemma stared at him, unable to believe her ears. Didn't he know how many years one had to train to be a teacher? Had he never heard of the independence of modern women who liked to earn their own living and not be dependent on their families for every penny they received? Didn't he know that few families could afford the luxury of keeping their womenfolk in idleness merely to prove the breadwinning abilities of their men? And a good thing too! How would he like to have nothing to do all the days of his life?

But she kept her thoughts to herself. What did it matter to her what this man thought? She looked down again at the letter, wondering why so many continental people chose to write on squared paper rather than the plain, unlined paper that most English people chose. It made her grandmother seem more of a foreigner to her than ever.

"Are you going to make the tea?" she asked instead. "Or is that women's work like bringing babies into the world?"

She wished she were less conscious of his hard, muscled body and, most of all, of the disapproving look in his eyes. It gave her a funny feeling inside. Perhaps it was that he appeared so uncompromisingly male. She shivered inwardly, thinking more kindly of the young men who had dated her and who had listened to her views on life with evident respect. They had never made her feel that she had no other use than to be female and subservient. Young men like Freddie Harmon whom she was almost sure was going to ask her to marry him that very evening. She conjured him up in her mind as if he were a touchstone to give her courage, but his face looked pale and uninteresting beside the dark features of the man in front of her, and honesty compelled her to admit that Freddie had never made her feel like much of a woman, not even when he had kissed her good night and tried to come inside with her for what he called a "nightcap."

"I'll make the tea," she sighed. "Won't you sit

down?" Perhaps he would be a little less of a challenge seated in her father's old chair.

"Thank you," he said.

He picked up her discarded shoes and put them neatly together out of his way, seating himself in the chair she had indicated. Standing, she had known him to be shorter than either her father or Freddie, seated, he lost even that one disadvantage and the very air crackled with the electricity he seemed to release into the atmosphere.

Gemma disappeared into the kitchen, glad to be out of his sight. There was a looking glass hanging beside the back door and she glanced at herself in it, annoyed to discover that her hair was about to come down and that her face was totally innocent of any of the makeup she had dabbed on in the common room before leaving school. No wonder he thought she looked a mess!

She undid her hair, letting it fall about her shoulders while she put the kettle on to boil. It was too heavy to contain in the severe style she had chosen for herself, but despite its despised coloring she was too vain to have it cut short. She liked the feel of its weight and abundance.

She saw his face in the mirror behind hers with no feeling of surprise. She surrendered the comb into his hand, scarcely daring to breathe. The touch of his fingers against hers was like an electric shock.

"One doesn't wear one's best clothes at school you know," she informed him severely.

"You are too old to go to school, *piccina.*"

"I go to teach, not to learn."

"What a waste of time when you have so much to learn," he mocked her.

She turned to face him, her eyes as green as grass. "I'll have you know I'm a fully qualified teacher with a certificate to prove it, so I can't have that much to learn!"

"No?"

How long could one survive without drawing breath? Her lips parted and she almost choked over the air that came in against her paralyzed throat. With relief she saw that the kettle was boiling.

"Excuse me," she said. "You do still want tea, don't you?"

"*Prego.* I am glad to see you have remembered your duties as hostess. Thank you, I shall be pleased to take tea with you."

"I—I'll just go upstairs and tidy up," she said quickly. He had not kissed her, but she knew it had been in his mind to do so and her own reactions were so mixed that she preferred to sort them out in the privacy of her bedroom. She snatched her comb from him, shaking the long mane of waving hair back over her shoulders. "I'm going out this evening. I—I think I'll change now to save time later."

"Going out? With whom?"

She wrinkled up her nose at him. "Does it matter?"

"Of course," he said seriously. "Would your grandmother approve of your escort, do you think? Was he known to your father?"

Gemma cast him an incredulous look. "Of course he was known to my father. He met him several times on the garden path in my company, and once—" her eyes shone with triumph—"once he came across him kissing me in the garden shed."

She didn't wait to see what his reaction would be to

that. But why should he think that Giulia had been the
only one who was attractive to the opposite sex?

She changed into a dress that Giulia had given her
shortly before her death. Gemma didn't really like it
for it drained her of the little color she had and turned
her golden hair a peculiar shade of green. But it was
made of real, wild silk and had a gorgeous sheen, and
Gemma could never have afforded anything as expensive. She looked through her shoes. Most of them were
practical rather than pretty. Teaching on her feet all day
had forced her to abandon her beloved high heels. She
did have one pair though, thrust into the back of the
cupboard. She pulled them out and looked at them,
undecided whether to wear them or not, but they were
pretty—and *that man*—

The dress definitely didn't suit her. She tore it off and
searched through the cupboard again. The only other
one she had that was suitable was made of black lace
over a wispy petticoat that only pretended to cover the
parts of her that mattered. It too had been Giulia's
dress in the first place, and Gemma gasped as she saw
how revealing it was of her own charms. It outlined her
shape in a way that brought the color to her cheeks and
the plunging neckline left very little to the imagination
as to the shape of her rounded breasts. But why not?
she thought, she wasn't ashamed of the way she looked!

Even so, it took courage to walk down the stairs and
pretend to herself she looked exactly the same as she
had when she had hurried up them. Marco Andreotti
was standing in the hall with the tea tray in his hands.
He looked up at her and raised his eyebrows. From
above she could see the austere planes of his face in a
new light.

"Well?" she challenged him.

A smile tugged at the corner of his lips. "I can see why your friend kissed you," he remarked, "but why in the garden shed?"

She descended the stairs, swinging her hips as she went. There was no reason that she could see why she should enlighten him.

"Where do you kiss your girl friends?" she asked him. "In a gondola?"

He put the tray down on a table by the sofa and turned his head to look at her again, appreciating her every curve with a long, low whistle. When he straightened up, however, the very masculine approval was gone from his eyes.

"That dress looked fine on your sister, Gemma *mia*," he told her, "but on you—" He spread his hands in an expressive gesture. "I would prefer your young man did not see you dressed like that," he finished severely.

"Oh would you?" she said. "But then it has nothing to do with you, has it? Besides, if it was all right on Giulia, why shouldn't it be all right on me?"

He turned down the corners of his mouth and raised his shoulders in what was almost an apology. "You are as different from your sister as chalk is from cheese. She knew herself as a woman and you do not. You will get your pretty wings singed."

Gemma flinched. Again, she was being compared to her more attractive sister! And by this obviously experienced man! A thought occurred to her. "Did you know Giulia in Venice? Did you like her?"

"Did you?" he countered.

She was shaken by the question. "Yes, I liked her," she answered doubtfully, "but not many women did.

Every man loved her though. She expected them to, and they did."

"But I did not," he said in such decisive tones that it would never have occurred to her to doubt him. "I like the promise of the bud better than the full-blown rose, which is why you will do me the favor of changing your dress once more. Have you nothing which is not a castoff of your sister's? Never mind, your grandmother can take you shopping in Venice and buy something more suitable for your age and coloring."

"And who will pay?" Gemma asked him faintly. "I doubt that she will and I most certainly can't."

"That is between your grandmother and myself and is no concern of yours." He seated himself on the edge of the sofa. "Will you please pour the tea, Gemma, before you go upstairs again. I like my tea with both milk and sugar, in the English way, one might say."

Gemma poured it out for him in silence. She hoped it poisoned him. She hoped the sugar would make him fat and unattractive. She hoped he'd never know how close he had come to having the whole lot poured over his sleek, black head.

It was only when she gained the landing once again that it occurred to her to wonder if Giulia had liked him. She began to laugh delightedly to herself because she was almost sure that Giulia had not. If she were not mistaken, Marco Andreotti was the "horrid boy who had lived in a tiny apartment at the poor end of the *calle*," and when had Giulia ever been known to like anyone who was poor?

Chapter Two

Nothing about Freddie Harmon pleased Gemma that evening. He complimented her upon her dress and she knew he was being insincere; she knew the color didn't suit her. What would he have thought of the black lace number if he could make himself ridiculous over the wild silk reject of Giulia's? Gemma was not sorry that Marco Andreotti had made her change, though she wished he had gone about it in a different way. The Italian made her nervous and she didn't like that. But Freddie seemed suddenly dull and predictable, and she was bored by his company, and even more bored by the prospect of becoming his wife.

"I'll give you all the time you need," Freddie was saying.

Gemma stopped thinking about the peculiar behavior of Marco Andreotti, recalling herself to her present surroundings with difficulty.

"All the time for what?"

Freddie looked hurt. His lower lip had a way of jutting out like a small boy's when something offended him. Gemma could well imagine that his mother had found it cute when he was a child but it was not attractive in a man, she reflected.

"Darling, I do wish you wouldn't interrupt," he complained. "I've been thinking about this all day. I know it's far too soon for you to decide. But you do know I'm here, waiting for you, don't you?"

Gemma tried to look grateful. "I may go to Italy to visit my grandmother," she said. "Or I may not."

"But Giulia didn't like her!"

"She wants me to go and see her."

"She never did before!"

"No, I suppose not, but Giulia was alive then and she had her. Now she has no one of her own, nor do I."

Freddie's lip jutted worse than ever, then his face cleared. "You can't go in the middle of the term, can you? We'll go together during the holidays."

"I don't know," Gemma said dubiously, "she has rather old-fashioned ideas, and supposing she doesn't approve of you, what then?"

"You haven't been listening, Gemma," he reproved her solemnly. "I've already explained to you that, although I really don't want to get married now, I'm prepared to put the date forward for your sake. It may even have some advantages—"

"Oh yes?"

"Well, I could move into your house, couldn't I? That would save on the rent. The house belongs to you, doesn't it? We wouldn't even have to pay off a mortgage as most young couples have to do."

Gemma stared at him. "And that's the only advantage you can see in marrying me?" she demanded.

"It's a big plus certainly," he agreed with self-satisfaction. "You haven't been working long enough to know how difficult it is to manage these days, but you'll soon find out. It was different when your father was alive."

"My father never paid a penny toward my training," Gemma told him. "He liked his job, but he never made much money. He paid for Giulia, but there wasn't enough left for me. Anyway, I preferred to do it all on my own."

"You have it all now."

Gemma looked at him, wondering that he should seem so strange and distant to her, as though he were someone she had known a long, long time ago in the past, and not very well at that.

"What do you suppose the all amounts to? A small fortune? It was mostly debts and a house I can't afford to live in. There were two funerals to pay for, apart from anything else, and my father didn't believe in taking out much insurance. He still thought of himself as being young—we all did."

"Not very practical," Freddie remarked. "But he must have left you something to live on? He was always free with his money where Giulia was concerned."

"I wonder?" Funny, Gemma thought, that she had never questioned her father's apparent largess toward her sister before. She had always concluded that it was he who had paid for her many trips to Venice, for the clothes she had acquired there, as well as for the

expensive training that was supposed to turn her
frivolous sister into a hardworking photographic
model.

"Who else paid for her?"

"Perhaps Nonna did."

"Your grandmother?"

Gemma nodded. "I know very little about her, but
Giulia always went to see her every year. She intended
leaving Giulia all her property—some decrepit house in
Venice that nothing will induce her to leave, and a small
interest in a Venetian glass factory. Giulia didn't think
it was going to make her fortune. She used to laugh
about her expectations, saying it was hardly worth
having to spend all her summer holidays among the
smelly canals of Venice. She didn't find it a romantic
city at all."

"But you do?"

Gemma nodded again. "I've never been there, but
I'd love to see it all. I'd love to be serenaded in a
gondola."

Freddie snorted. "Expensive nonsense!"

"I'd still enjoy it."

"Not with me you won't! I have better things on
which to spend my money."

She knew what he spent his money on. His rooms
were full of electrical gadgets, half-a-dozen radios and,
what she had always considered to be eccentric, two
color televisions which he kept permanently tuned to
different stations. She had always been amused by that
in the past but, suddenly, she wasn't amused by it
anymore. Imagine living with that noise all one's life!

"I think I'd like to go home now," she said abruptly.

"Don't you want to dance?"

She shook her head. "Not tonight. It—it hasn't been an easy day today and I'm tired."

"But you're never tired!" he objected.

She sniffed disparagingly. "I am tonight!" Anyone would be, she told herself, after dealing with that Italian. It would be a long time before she forgot that he had told her she looked like a mess.

"Come on then, I'll take you home," Freddie offered awkwardly. "You look tired. It isn't like you to be in the doldrums for a whole evening." He sounded sulky and Gemma wondered which particular electrical gadget he had planned to tell her about that evening. He didn't care that she understood nothing about any of his enthusiasms, but he did expect her to listen to everything he had to say.

Only tonight she had wanted to talk about Marco Andreotti. She still couldn't believe that any man would be arrogant enough to correct her manners, to openly disapprove of her neglect of her grandmother and, worst of all, to order her about in her own home as if he had known her all her life instead of a few minutes.

Freddie wanted to take her home on the bus. "If we're going to be married we'll have to save all our pennies from now on," he muttered, lengthening his stride against the gusts of wind that blew down the street.

"I want to go home in a taxi," Gemma insisted.

"My dear girl—"

"I can't walk in these shoes."

"Then what did you put them on for?"

To impress Marco Andreotti! "I'm tired of solid, sensible shoes!" She was surprised to hear that she sounded both exasperated and angry. "I wanted it to be a lovely evening."

"You're too romantic for your own good, Gemma. The kind of thing you want is once in a lifetime stuff. We know each other too well for that kind of thing."

Was that what was wrong? Gemma didn't know. What she did know was that she wasn't going to walk another step! She hailed a taxi with a piercing whistle, ignoring Freddie's shocked look. One of London's black, square taxicabs drew up beside her, the driver grinning at her.

"Where to, Miss?"

"Are you coming, Freddie?"

Freddie stood in the middle of the road, clinking his change in his pocket. She knew he was thinking that if he went with her he would have to pay. Finally, he shook his head. "I think I'll walk," he said.

Gemma had a particular affection for London after dark. She liked its cosmopolitan atmosphere and she always felt its excitement. The Queen's standard was flying over Buckingham Palace and Queen Victoria's statue watched the foot guards standing at attention behind the black and gilded railings. Then, almost immediately, they were in Westminster and were racing across the bridge to the district where Gemma lived, just south of the river.

"It's on the corner there," she pointed out her house to the driver. "Just beyond that pillar-box."

He put her down outside the entrance to the pocket-handkerchief strip of garden that so many London houses have in the front, taking her five-pound note and giving her back remarkably little change.

She didn't know when she noticed the light on in the

house. She tried to call to the taxi driver to come back, but he was already skimming round the corner intent on getting back to the West End and more customers. Had she left the light on? She didn't think so, though she had been in such a rush when Marco Andreotti had finally gone that she might have done anything.

She took out her key and opened the front door, kicking off her shoes as she did so.

"Is anybody there?" she called out, feeling like a fool. What burglar was likely to answer such a foolish question?

The landing light came on, followed by the one in the hall, and Marco Andreotti came slowly down the stairs toward her.

"Good heavens!" she exclaimed. Her throat felt dry and her heart was beating so hard against her ribs she was sure he could hear it. "What in the world are you doing here?"

He was wearing a terry dressing gown and his black hair was wet as if he had just stepped out of the shower.

"I didn't mean to frighten you," he apologized. "Where is the boy friend?"

Gemma threaded her fingers together in dismay. How like Freddie not to be there when she most needed him.

"I came home alone," she said.

"Afraid he'll keep you company all night?"

"Certainly not! Freddie isn't—isn't like that!" She eyed him suspiciously. "I hope you're not either," she added.

"It sounds as though you had a disappointing evening," he taunted her. "You're home earlier than I expected—"

"How did you get in?" she demanded.

He put out a hand and touched the shining chignon at the nape of her neck. "How could he let you come home alone?" he asked her.

"I came by taxi. They're expensive these days. *How did you get in?*"

"Through the back door. I left it open earlier."

One by one the pins that held her hair in place were being removed and she did nothing about it. She stood, head meekly bent, trying to control the emotions at war in her breast.

"*Anyone* could have gotten in!" she exclaimed.

"But anyone didn't," he pointed out. "Besides, I knew I wouldn't be gone for long."

"Why go at all then?"

"Someone had to tell your school you won't be going back there—"

Her head came up with a jolt. "How dare you?" she shot at him. "If you don't leave at once, I'll call the police! And I hope no one believed you at school because I shall be going back there, *every day* until the end of the term. Where I won't be going is to Venice! I shall go and see Nonna during the holidays, when Freddie can come with me. Nothing would induce me to go anywhere with you!"

"It would look a little odd if I left here in my dressing gown," he answered, unperturbed by her anger. He even had the audacity to smile. "You'll have to wait until I'm properly dressed before you turn me out—*if* you turn me out."

"You can't stay here!"

"Why not? How many beds does one girl need for a good night's sleep?"

Gemma clenched her fists. "That isn't the point. The point is that I'm alone in the house—"

"And your grandmother would disapprove?"

"I don't care if she does or not!" Gemma declared, finally losing her temper. "It's what I think that matters to me."

"Is it?" His dark eyes mocked her. "Is that why you wear your sister's castoffs?"

Gemma drew herself up with dignity. "That's unkind," she protested. "Giulia had more clothes than I because she needed more. A model does. And if she passed on some of the ones she no longer wanted to me, it was very kind of her. As a family we've always had to be careful what we spent. I'm not ashamed of it. How else would I have come by a dress made from wild silk?"

"It doesn't become you in the least."

Her green eyes flashed. "What's that to you?"

He ran an impatient hand through his hair. "I like my women to be elegant and beautiful. Believe me, I know what it is to be poor. I never saw my mother dressed in anything else but black, a dull, rusty black that made her look as shapeless and as old as all the other widows who live in the poor parts of Venice. Your grandmother never looked like that! She was a widow too, but she always looked cool and as if her clothes were brand new. She smelled nice too. My people always smelled of cooking and fish!"

"So what?" Gemma asked crossly. "I'm proud to smell of chalk and the classroom. I expect your mother had to work and my grandmother didn't."

"What do you know about her?" he sneered. "For God's sake get out of that dress before I tear it off your

back, and then come back here and I'll tell you about
your grandmother. You ought to know something
about her before you meet her face to face." He thrust
a hand into her hair, jerking her face up to meet the fire
in his eyes. "Heaven knows what she's going to make of
you."

"I'm going to marry Freddie and live in London, so
what difference does it make what she thinks!"

Another jerk on the rope of her hair brought the
tears into her eyes. He let her go, shaking his head with
a violence that hypnotized her even while she longed to
make good her escape upstairs to the privacy of her
bedroom.

"You had better put all such thoughts out of your
mind until after you have seen your grandmother," he
said dryly. "She has other plans for you."

His face was drained of all emotion. It frightened her
more than anything he could have said to her. It was an
austere face, with heavy, drooping eyelids; the face of a
man accustomed to having his own way, who issued
orders rather than received them and who expected
them to be obeyed instantly.

"Freddie is not for you," he said at last. "He hasn't
even the guts to kiss you good night!"

She opened her eyes very wide. "How do you
know?" she challenged him.

"Because you hadn't been kissed when you came in
here, frightened and *alone!*"

"You can't know that!" she protested. "And anyway,
it doesn't alter the fact that I'm engaged to marry
Freddie. I love him very much."

"Do you?" The glint in his eyes spelled danger, but

she ignored the warning. "Do you really, Miss Gemma Savage?"

"Yes, I do!"

She had thought his mouth cruel, but it wasn't. It was warm and persuasive and very, very insistent. Her own lips parted beneath his, all thought, all movement completely suspended. She had never been kissed like this before. Her nostrils were filled with the smell of the shampoo he had used on his hair and the warm, wet, masculine smell of his body under its inadequate covering. Her hair swung like a curtain about them and patches of damp showed clearly on her dress where Marco had held her close up against himself.

"Now you look kissed!" he said with satisfaction, releasing her so abruptly that her knees nearly gave way under her.

Belatedly, she realized she was still clutching at the collar of his dressing gown, pulling it away from his neck and revealing the smooth brown skin of his chest and shoulders. She would have liked to have put her lips against that skin and then to have kissed him again, swept off her feet and given no choice but to submit to his greater strength and determination. *What was the matter with her?* Marco Andreotti was a very experienced man—that was obvious—who had known countless women in the past and who was not to be relied on to behave in a normal, civilized manner. Well, she would soon show him that it had meant as little to her as it had meant to him!

She opened her mouth to speak, but could think of nothing whatever to say.

"I'm going upstairs. When I come down again I

expect you to be out of this house and *never* to come back!"

"Poor Freddie," he remarked.

She turned on her heel, her face hidden from him by the curtain of her loosened hair. "Why do you say that?" she demanded.

"He'll never know what to make of the Italian side to you. It beats me how you've hidden it so successfully for so long—from yourself mostly, I suspect."

"Will you get out of my house?" Her voice rose on an hysterical note that appalled her. She had always prided herself on being cool and calm in the face of the enemy.

"And spend a night in the park?" A smile broke across his face and she was astonished to see that he was trying not to laugh. "London is full to bursting and very expensive besides. I tried one or two hotels and then I gave up. Besides, I like it here," he added meaningfully.

"You're not staying here."

It sounded more like a question than a statement. What could she do about it if he did decide to stay? She had some experience now of the strength of his muscles and, although she was reasonably strong for a woman, what woman had ever won against a determined man?

She tried again. "*Signore,* why are you doing this to me? Is it to get your revenge because Giulia disliked you so thoroughly?"

His crack of laughter released a rush of adrenalin into her blood.

"What makes you think Giulia disliked me?" he asked.

She chewed on her lower lip. "She said she did. You are the boy who lived at the other end of the *calle*, aren't you? She always hated you." Gemma looked down her nose at him. "I don't think she approved of your friendship with Nonna. She thought it strange that a young boy would hang round in the company of an elderly woman, unless it was her money you were after?"

"She hasn't got any."

That was what Gemma had concluded also. "Then you didn't even have that excuse?" she pressed him.

"Do I need an excuse before befriending your grandmother? She is a very charming old lady and, of her family, only Giulia ever came to see her. A granddaughter who was as English as her looks were Italian, and who despised Donna Maria because she lived in the past, in the midst of a decaying grandeur that Giulia didn't understand. She was always advising the old lady to sell her family's pictures, to dispose of all her precious ornaments, to let the *palazzo* fall into the canal in peace, and to go and live in one of those blocks of apartments built of concrete, glass, and stainless steel, and which have as much to recommend them as her own greedy little soul. Of course she wanted to dislike me. Donna Maria and I would talk all the time of how we would one day restore the *palazzo* to its former glory. Giulia may not have understood her grandmother but at least she came every year—each one as more of a favor than the last! Where were you?"

Gemma's hands shook. "I was here," she said. "No one ever suggested that I should go to Venice."

"But you're going now?"

She took another step up the stairs. "I'll go and see her if she wants me to, but not with you! I never want to see you again!"

She could feel his eyes on her back, but she would not look round, she would not.

"Go to bed, Gemma *mia*. I promise not to disturb you until morning."

Not disturb her? When he had already done everything he could to destroy her peace of mind? And where was he going to sleep? She was not going to make up a bed for him.

"I'm in your father's room," he said as if he had read her thoughts, "just in case you need me," he added maliciously.

She turned and faced him then, her head held high. "I'll never need you!" she declared with heat. "You flatter yourself, *signore!*"

"Perhaps, *signorina,* it is not a point I will argue. Go to bed, Gemma, or are you waiting for me to kiss you good night?"

How she would have liked to slap him, but she didn't dare. Who knew what he would do to her then? Instead, she mounted the stairs with a straight back and unhurried steps, making a mad dash for her room as soon as she was out of his sight, firmly shutting and locking her door behind her.

Chapter Three

Gemma rolled over with a groan. Was it morning already?

"A cup of tea, *signorina?*"

Her eyes focused with difficulty on Marco Andreotti's dark face. She stared at him in silence for a moment and then hoisted herself angrily up in the bed.

"You have no right to come in here!" she began. Surely she had locked her bedroom door? "How did you get in?"

He held the key out, dangling it in front of her nose. "I dislike locked doors," he said.

"Oh do you? And what has it got to do with you what I do in my own house? If I want to lock my door—"

"Everything to do with you has to do with me," he

answered her. He sat down on the edge of her bed and poured out two cups of tea, handing one of them to her.

He was still dressed in the terry dressing gown, though he had had the grace to put a pair of pajama trousers on underneath it. That brought her thoughts back to herself and what *she* was wearing. To her relief she remembered she was clad in a demure nightgown that reached all the way from neck to toes, and even had pretty little bows of ribbon at the neck and wrists. She took a deep breath, preparing to do further battle with him.

"Are you a burglar by profession?" she asked him politely.

His eyes mocked her. "Does it matter to you?"

She shrugged. "As breaking and entering seems to be your normal mode of getting in—"

His eyebrows lifted, doing funny things to her breathing. "When have I broken anything?" he demanded. "All your windows are intact. Your doors have not been wrenched open. I have trespassed on your hospitality possibly, but I have done you no more harm than that!"

"Is that all?" she retorted dryly.

"What other harm have I done you?"

What more harm had he done? He seemed to have taken over her whole life!

"Well, one thing you've done is to show me that the locks on the doors of this house are totally inadequate. If you can get in and out at will, so can anyone else. I shall have all the locks changed this very day!"

"You'll have no time for that sort of thing today. That's why I woke you. It's almost time for us to leave for the airport."

Her mouth set in a stubborn line. "It is almost time for me to leave to go to work!" she retorted.

"Not today, Gemma Savage." He picked a lock of hair from her cheek and pushed it back behind her ear. Her pulses drummed dangerously at his touch and she stopped breathing altogether, lest he should see how disturbing she was finding this interview. "Your Headmistress was most understanding that you needed time off to visit your only surviving relative. She was concerned that you had gone on working when the accident happened. Even the funerals were arranged for a Saturday so that you wouldn't have to take time off, weren't they?"

"I take my work seriously," she agreed primly.

"At the expense of everything else? I shall have to teach you the priorities in your life, Gemma *mia*. It is more than time that you considered the welfare of your grandmother and, for that, you need to go to Venice."

Gemma stared mutinously at her rapidly cooling cup of tea. "What makes you think my grandmother wants to see me? She never did before!"

"She never insisted you visit her before," Marco contradicted her, a hard edge to his voice. "But now that you are alone there are no more excuses as to why you should stay away from her. Cheer up, Gemma, you may find you like Venice better than you think."

"Giulia never did."

"No." A look of scorn crossed his face. "Like you, she only saw her grandmother's life from her own point of view. You made a selfish, spoiled pair who should have been smacked into a better frame of mind when you were children. It's too late for your sister, but it's not too late for you!"

She was outraged. "I don't believe in lifting a hand to any child. Nor did my father. I—I think it's contemptible of you to say such things about us when you don't know anything about us! And I'm not going to Venice today, and most certainly not with you!"

He took her cup out of her hand and put it down on the tray. She lay there, frozen to the spot, wondering what was coming next. His expression was unreadable, his eyes veiled by his heavy lids. She began to panic. She could feel her heart pounding against her ribs and she began to worry that he would hear it for himself. He put a hand under her chin, turning her face toward him.

"You have half an hour to dress and pack," he said.

"I'm not going with you!" She was trembling now.

"You will do as you're told!"

He sounded so certain, so sure of himself and of his power to make her do as he wanted. She licked her lips nervously, wishing she had the strength of mind to brush his hand away.

"I—"

He put his mouth against hers in a kiss so light that she couldn't be sure she hadn't imagined it.

"Half an hour," he repeated. "If you are not ready, I'll dress you and pack for you myself. Understand?"

She gulped and nodded. She believed every word he said.

"I hate you!" she said.

His lips twitched at the corners. "Hate me all you like, Gemma *mia,* you'll still be on that plane for Venice today with me beside you." He shrugged his shoulders, his dark eyes shining with amusement.

"Besides, a woman's hatred—it is as fitful as a summer storm, a great deal of noise and a few flashes of temperament. Hate me all you please, *ma bella,* it makes no difference to me."

Her breasts rose and fell in increasing agitation. There was no dealing with this man! He had no right, who did he think he was?

"Oh, go away—" she commanded him bitterly. *"Mi lasci stare!"* she added in Italian for good measure. "Leave me alone!"

He prepared to leave, but changed his mind at the last moment. "You have a very good accent in Italian," he commended her. "Who taught you to speak your mother's language?"

She cast him a sulky look. "I learned at school."

"I thought most English schools taught only French?"

"I wanted to learn Italian. It had—it had nothing to do with my mother's nationality. I never even knew her."

He took a step toward the door and then paused again. "Did Giulia learn Italian also?"

She refused to answer but, when he showed no signs of leaving until she did, she said reluctantly, "Giulia was not much good at languages. In fact she didn't like school much at all. I did."

"So much that you took up teaching so that you wouldn't have to leave your schooldays behind you?" he taunted her.

She shook her head. "I like teaching, and it's something I do well. I value my independence, something which I don't expect you to understand. A teacher in this country is paid at the expense of the State, not of her parents. My father never had to pay a penny for any of my education."

He explored her shape under the bedclothes, a flicker of amusement in his eyes. "You look like a fully grown woman, but you're still an adolescent underneath, aren't you? Pig-headed and spoiled."

"At least I mind my own business!" she flared up.

"Isn't your grandmother your business?" he countered.

She sighed. "She seems to be more yours than mine," she said dryly. "Why don't you take care of her? You know her much better than I do."

"But it's her granddaughter she wants," he answered calmly. "Everything I want to do for her depends on you."

"And what will Nonna have to say about the way you marched into my house, picked the lock of my bedroom door, and—and—"

"And kissed you good night?"

Her cheeks burned. "I don't suppose you'd want me to tell her that," she demurred.

"Tell her if you want to," he invited her. "I can always tell her how you kissed me back!"

Her eyes became enormous pools of green. "Oh, I did not!" she denied.

His laughter undermined what little self-confidence she had left. "Don't tempt me, Gemma," he advised her, with more gentleness than she had heard from him all morning, "not unless you're prepared to face the consequences."

She felt a glimmer of triumph. "Men always blame women for tempting them when they're in the wrong," she declared grandly. "You kissed me all by your-self."

"It was a pity you didn't tell me how reluctant you were at the time," he remarked. "Next time you'd better slap my face rather than cling to my collar."

Her moment of triumph died away. "That'll be the day!" she said nastily.

"Won't it though?" he echoed. "You won't be slapping me, will you, Gemma?"

She jerked her chin upward. "I don't believe in it."

"So you said before. How little you know yourself. Savage by name and savage by nature. The only thing that gives you pause, my Gemma, is the thought that I might be the man to force you to look at yourself as you really are. It might be a pleasurable discovery."

"Not if you have anything to do with it!"

"Poor Gemma," he mocked her. "Did you dislike my kissing you so much?"

She was thankful he would never know the answer to that. She was ashamed that he could even think that she might have enjoyed his embrace and even more ashamed that it could have been her own actions which had given him that impression. There was no doubt that Marco Andreotti was very experienced in trifling with young women, but he would have to learn that she was not the easy prey he thought she was. And who was going to teach him? a small voice asked in her mind. He had accused her of kissing him back, *and she had!* And, what's more, she wouldn't have objected if he had kissed her again! She couldn't even be sure she would object if he were to kiss her again right now, which was ridiculous, because she didn't like him at all. He was far too sure of himself.

If she were wise, she would send him back to Venice empty-handed, to make what excuses he cared to as to why he had returned to her grandmother alone. But she wanted to go to Venice. She wanted to see her grandmother. And more than anything else, she wanted to teach Marco Andreotti a lesson he would never forget.

She bounced out of bed and dressed herself in the first clothes that came to hand: a pair of green corduroy jeans and a jacket to match, clothes which she had chosen for herself and which accentuated the clear green of her eyes. If she only had half an hour in which to pack her things, she would have to hurry.

Although she had read much about Venice and seen pictures of the most famous landmarks of the city, the many canals—the streets of water—still came as a surprise to Gemma.

"Welcome to Venice," Marco said, as he helped her into the tiny motorboat that he used as another man in another city would have used his personal, chauffeur-driven car. She noticed he was actually smiling. "You look very much at home here," he remarked.

"But I'm not used to boats," she said shyly.

"Half the ladies of Venice could say the same," he told her. "They always have to be helped in and out although they've been doing it all their lives. If you see a woman rowing herself, you can be sure she's a foreigner."

Gemma sniffed. She didn't like to say she thought his compatriots poor-spirited, but as the comment was written plainly on her face she might just as well have done so. His smile grew broader.

"Wait until you've escorted your grandmother across

the city half-a-dozen times! She has the same antipathy toward water as have our Venetian cats."

Gemma's attention was caught by the numerous representations of lions she could see all around her. "Why so many lions?" she asked, "and why is the lion considered particularily the emblem of Venice?" The boat swayed ominously in the wake of another.

"Saint Mark is always represented by a lion."

"Ah yes," she observed, "his body was stolen by the Venetians and brought here, like so much else in Venice, wasn't it?"

He didn't resent the accusation. "If the many pictures about the city are to be believed, Saint Mark himself welcomed the change of scene. We have never doubted that he takes his duties as our patron saint very seriously."

Gemma was amused. "Does he watch over you as carefully?" she asked.

"I've never thought to ask him. So far, I've been content to live in his shadow, as we all in Venice live in the shadow of his great cathedral."

"The lion's shadow," she said.

His eyes glinted. And then, at her look of inquiry, he quoted, *"Beware your name's not Thisbe,"* he warned her. *"In such a night did Thisbe fearfully o'ertrip the dew, And saw the lion's shadow ere himself, And ran dismay'd away."*

"I'm made of sterner stuff," she declared. "Why should I take fright at a mere shadow?"

"Why indeed?" he murmured.

But she was afraid. She was afraid of him and the effect he had on her, and she was afraid of herself. A few minutes in Venice and she scarcely recognized herself as being the same person who lived in that small, shabby, London house and taught school every day. This stranger was a langorous being, content to be transported along the canals of Venice, without lifting a finger herself. She was full of sun, and strange sights and sounds, and there was a spice to sparring with Marco Andreotti that she could enjoy when they were not alone and there was no danger of things getting out of hand. In public she could tease him to her heart's content.

The Grand Canal had practically come to a standstill, so thick was the traffic that churned its way through its waters.

"What is that smell?" Gemma inquired, wrinkling up her nose.

"Half drainage, half rotting stone," Marco told her. "You'd better get used to it. The *palazzo* smells like that all the time."

"But don't the authorities do anything about it?"

"They try. Fortunately we have a tide here which washes away much of the refuse, but it's too expensive to give Venice a proper drainage system. Many of the canals date from the ninth century, and we use the same means now as they used then to clean them. About every twenty years, the canals are drained and the fetid mud at the bottom is dug out with a shovel."

Gemma, whose hygienic standards were somewhat more modern than those of the ninth century, was frankly horrified.

"You mean they haven't thought of anything else to do about it?"

He laughed. "Most houses have septic tanks nowadays. That's quite a step forward."

Gemma might have told him exactly what she thought of such archaic arrangements. As it was, she merely changed the subject. "Do you know that girl standing on that bridge? She seems to be trying to attract your attention."

Marco glanced up at the girl in question. Gemma eyed him curiously, noting with interest the slight tightening of his mouth and the quick way he veiled his eyes with his heavy lids.

"She is not somebody I wish to introduce you to," he said repressively.

"Why not?" she demanded. She thought the girl elegant in a way that she was quickly coming to recognize as the hallmark of Venetian women. "Shall I wave back to her?"

"She is not a suitable friend for you." His voice was as expressionless as his face.

"I believe you know her very well indeed, so why shouldn't I know her too?" Gemma was delighted to have found something which plainly ran deep with him. At last, she thought, she could get her own back on him and have her revenge for the disparaging way he had spoken of Freddie Harmon.

"I think you know very well why it isn't suitable for you to befriend her," he said mildly.

Gemma couldn't resist a grin. "I'm a very modern girl! We are quite permissive in our ideas now in England. I thought you were in Italy too? Besides," she added, "she looks nice!" Her eyes danced with amusement at his obvious embarrassment. "What's her name?"

"Gisela."

"Almost one of the family!" Gemma approved. "My

mother wanted all our names to begin with the same
initial. If I had had another sister, she might well have
been called Gisela. She even looks a little like Giulia,
don't you think?"

"No, I don't."

"Perhaps it's only that Giulia looked so Italian. I
used to long to be dark and mysterious, instead of being
blond and tall with it!"

Marco's eyes met hers and their impact was such that
she looked away hastily.

"Not all Italians are small and dark," Marco said
softly. "You inherited more from your mother than you
know."

She shook her head, still not looking at him. "I'm
English through and through. Everybody's always said
so!"

Her attention was diverted by their branching off the
Grand Canal and darting down a series of narrower,
lesser canals, until she hadn't the faintest idea where
she was.

"There's the *palazzo* over there," Marco pointed out
to her.

Gemma's first emotion was that of disappointment.
Giulia had never referred to their grandmother's home
as a palace, but Marco had, ever since he had first
mentioned it and, unconsciously, she had thought of it
as being built of marble, something as splendid as
Blenheim Palace, or the chateaux of the Loire, and this
was no more than a terra-cotta building, with tall,
balconied windows, all of which looked as if they were
about to fall into the water below, and a roof of pantiles
that was badly in need of repair.

"It could do with a coat of paint, couldn't it?" Gemma remarked, swallowing hard.

"It could indeed," he agreed. "And that's not all that's wrong with it. Your grandmother won't allow me to put it in order for her though until it belongs to me. She is a very proud old lady."

"It won't be much of an inheritance," Gemma said.

"You haven't seen the inside yet. When I was a boy, I used to dream of owning my own *palazzo* in Venice."

"No wonder Giulia didn't want it!" Gemma muttered.

Marco clenched his teeth until the muscles in his cheeks stood out. Gemma guessed that he didn't like to hear any criticism of the *palazzo*, and wondered if her grandmother would feel the same way. It would be hard not to be disparaging about the cracking facade and the sun-blistered shutters on the windows.

Their boat was tied up to one of the poles that stood outside the main door. These poles had once been scarlet and white, but the paint had peeled away long ago, leaving them silvered and covered with an unhealthy green slime. Marco stepped ashore and reached down a hand to her, pulling her out of the boat and to his side. The door was enormous and she felt dwarfed by it. It was like the entrance to a cathedral, arched and studded with rusting wrought-iron symbols.

Marco pushed open a smaller door that had been cut into one side of this magnificent portal and stepped over the bar at the bottom.

"Welcome home," he said.

It was dark inside, but not too dark to see the damp patches that covered the stone floor, or the duckboards that had been thoughtfully provided to keep one's shoes dry.

"I don't believe it!" Gemma exclaimed. "Is it sinking, or what?"

Marco was unconcerned. "It only happens at certain times of the year. In the summer we move back downstairs, but in the winter we live upstairs. I'll take you upstairs now. Your grandmother will be waiting to meet you."

But Gemma hung back. She needed time to get used to this moldy house of her grandmother's before she was taken to see its owner.

Her nervousness was reinforced by the marble staircase that rose out of the entrance hall without any visible means of support. The bannisters were too wide for her to grasp.

In the gloom upstairs several pictures had been hung. Most of them were as dark with age as their surroundings and painted in oils. Only one stood out from the others, a paper print that had been torn out of some magazine, representing the leonine symbol of the city, the canals and the Doge's Palace behind the long-maned beast whose paw was holding open a book.

"*Pax tibi Marce evangili sta meus,*" Gemma read aloud.

"Peace be unto you Mark my evangelist," Marco translated for her in an inscrutable voice. "The picture was given to me by my godfather when I made my first communion. I gave it to Donna Maria when we first became friends."

And her grandmother had appreciated the gift, Gemma thought, and had cared enough about her young friend to put the picture with all the others.

The floor creaked as she walked across the landing. Already awed by her surroundings, Gemma put out a hand and tugged at Marco's coat sleeve.

He nodded. "You don't have to be afraid of Donna Maria," he encouraged her. "She has never been known to bear a grudge against anyone. She certainly won't when she sees you!"

He pushed open a door at the end of the passage and thrust her into the room before him. A fire was burning in the enormous fireplace opposite the half-shuttered windows and someone was sitting in the leather chair that had been drawn up close to the warming blaze.

Gemma took a step forward and saw her grandmother for the first time. She was practically as tall a woman as she was·herself, and the same green eyes stared back at her, as astonished as her own. What her hair had been like when she had been young it was impossible to imagine, but now she wore a magnificent wig of long rippling hair, the color of golden syrup. She even had the same strange greenish tinge to her eyelids that had always caused Gemma such sorrow.

"Nonna?" she breathed.

"Gemma?" Her grandmother rose to her feet which were shod in the highest heels that Gemma had ever seen. "Oh, *Gemma!* Why did nobody ever tell me! My dearest girl, you are a Venetian to your fingertips. Darling Gemma, welcome home!"

Chapter Four

"Giulia should have told me!"

Aware that she had spoken at exactly the same time as her grandmother, Gemma made a gesture of apology. That they should have chosen to make the same exclamation in the same words struck her as mildly ridiculous. What had she in common with this aging lady in her blond wig after all? Perhaps she had once been as dark as Giulia had been.

"It is remarkable that she should have been hidden away from you all these years," Marco said with dry irony. "She wouldn't have come now if I hadn't forced her hand."

Gemma chewed on her lower lip. "Giulia was the image of Mama. We always thought of her as being the Italian one. She looked the part."

"Italian, yes," her grandmother agreed, "but Venetian, no. It is my blood you have in your veins, child. My family is Venetian to the core. Your mother took after her father. He was a Florentine, you know."

"But didn't he live here with you?" Gemma asked her.

"Of course," the old lady conceded. "I would not move from the *palazzo*, not even for him, and so he came to Venice to be with me. And here you are now, following in his footsteps. You are very welcome, Gemma *cara.*" Her grandmother's lips parted in a faint smile. "The more welcome," she added, "for being the image of myself at your age! I had not believed it possible! To have such looks is rare now even in the great Venetian families. How jealous all my friends will be when they see you!"

"But, Nonna, I won't be here for very long. It's the middle of the term, you see, and I have to get back if I want to go on teaching. I can't afford to get a reputation for being unreliable. It's very difficult—"

"Yes, yes," her grandmother acknowledged impatiently, "but you are here now and I mean to make the most of it. Marco, take Gemma up to the gallery so that she may see for herself how much she is one of the family. Once she has seen how all her ancestors share the same looks she will realize her place is among them and not teaching the children of other women. We have always bred well in my family and she has the right hips for childbirth, don't you agree, Marco?"

Gemma gave them both an outraged look. "You don't seem to have been very successful in recent generations!" she retorted. "At least Mama produced two girls to your one!"

"True, but I had two sons as well."

"Oh." Discomforted, Gemma sought support from Marco only to discover that he was still exploring the possibilities of her body with a languid air. His interest brought the color burning up into her cheeks and she turned her face away before he could see the effect he was having on her. "I didn't know I had any uncles," she said in a small voice.

"They were both killed in the war. They fought well and they died bravely. From then on I had only your mother until she went to England with your father. But now I have you!"

"You had Giulia," Gemma pointed out.

"A reluctant English girl with no feeling for her Venetian heritage. It would have been better if you had come in her place sometimes. I could have taught you much, little Gemma. She, I could teach nothing at all!"

It hurt Gemma to hear her sister dismissed in such terms. How could her grandmother have thought her English, when she and her father had always thought of her as being the Italian member of their family? Gemma couldn't remember her mother, but she had seen enough photographs of her to know how like her her sister had been. And what could her grandmother have taught her? Gemma had been English all her life and she had no ambition to discover a foreign, Venetian side to her nature.

"I am very well as I am!" she said aloud.

"You will see," her grandmother answered calmly. "Take her away, Marco, and show her the portraits. I am tired from so much excitement."

The man bent over the old lady's chair. "You are well, Donna Maria? You are not feeling ill?"

Her thin, brittle fingers patted his firm arm. "You are too good to me, Marco. I am content and that is enough for anyone at my age. Thank you for bringing my granddaughter to me."

He shrugged his shoulders. "As long as you are pleased—"

The old lady's eyes snapped. "Are you not pleased with her?" she demanded.

"I?" He smiled down at her. "She is well enough. Doubtless the Venetian air will improve her if she is here long enough."

"But—"

His eyes smiled down at her. "You must forgive me if I prefer her grandmother. I have known her longer you see and have known her kindness for many, many years."

They laughed together and Gemma felt shut out from their intimacy. It was a lonely feeling, though she couldn't think why it should disturb her, making her want to be a part of their circle. This was Giulia's world, not hers! And yet, to hear them talking, she knew that Giulia had always been a stranger among them. Gemma should have felt a stranger also, but a part of her was as much at home in her grandmother's presence as she had ever felt in her father's house. She felt a sudden sense of urgency to see her ancestors' portraits, to see if she recognized any part of herself in them. If she did, she might find she had more in common with the strange old woman who was her grandmother than she had thought. It was an appealing thought. It would be nice to have someone of her own again.

But she would never have anything in common with Marco! That would be asking too much. She followed him up another magnificent flight of stairs. Angry with herself when she realized that she had hardly glanced at her surroundings, so intent had she been on finding fault with the set of his wide shoulders and the lithe way he mounted the stairs.

The gallery smelled of neglect and rising damp. It was an enormous room, the ceilings rising almost out of sight. The windows were shuttered, but when Marco opened them, she could see they were narrow, with strange Gothic arches that had little to do with the architecture of the rest of the *palazzo*.

Marco turned and faced her. "Allow me to present you to your family," he mocked her openly. "I hope you are impressed to be a part of such an ancient lineage?"

"I've never thought about it," she said honestly. "What about your family? Aren't you Venetian through and through?"

"I am. My family did not supply the city with any of its Doges or other notables however. I trace my ancestors by word of mouth. This one was hanged for theft, that one never bothered to marry the mother of his children, and the most famous of them all was a glass blower who tried to escape from Venice and take his secrets elsewhere. For that he died on the scaffold also."

Gemma blinked, wishing she hadn't asked. "And what did these people do? Were they so much better?"

He put his hands on her shoulders and stood her face to face with a medieval version of her own self. "They

were richer," he remarked wryly. "And they paid for
dressing. The jewels appear as often as do the Venetian
golden looks."

Gemma frowned at one portrait after another. The
likeness among the women especially was quite extraor-
dinary. In earlier days they had worn their hair high,
training it through their crownless hats, like vines
through a trellis. Many of them had affected the high
clogs, some of them twenty inches high, which had
made it impossible for them to walk without a servant
to support them on either side.

"I can imagine Nonna fitting in very well with her,"
Gemma remarked once, pointing to one of the more
decadent looking ladies who was completely surrounded by a group of admiring young men. "They both have
the look of a courtesan."

If she had hoped to shock Marco, she was doomed to
disappointment. "Courtesans in the sixteenth century
were some of our most honored and admired citizens.
At the end of the century there were five times as many
of them as there were nuns in the city. Venetian women
have always had warm, loving natures."

Gemma sniffed. "But isn't that what courtesans are
not?" she argued. "Don't women become courtesans
because they can't sustain any more lasting relationship?"

"In those days," Marco said dryly, "one did not
marry for love."

Gemma raised her brows. "What about now?" she
asked.

A muscle twitched in his cheek. "I believe in the best
families the girls are only allowed to meet men whom

their parents consider to be possible marriage partners."

Gamma actually smiled. "How glad you must be to be considered unsuitable!" she murmured.

His heavy lids hid what he was thinking. "Times have changed, or you would not be alone with me now, Gemma Savage. I would have been considered far too dangerous a threat to your honor."

He could be that today, she thought. It was impossible to ever forget he was a man. She kept thinking that she didn't like him, but she had learned in the last twenty-four hours that one didn't have to like a man to be inwardly shaken by him. She had never felt herself to be more female and vulnerable than in the society of Marco Andreotti, and the sensation was one she would like to forget as quickly as possible.

"Yet that woman is alone with a whole bevy of young men," she objected, "none of them her husband by the look of them."

"She is not a young virgin, untried in the ways of love. When that portrait of her was painted, she had been a widow for several years and was the mother of several children. Here are two of her older children, her son and her eldest daughter."

The girl had mischievous green eyes that were a vivid reflection of Gemma's own; she shared the same golden looks, the flat, almost Slavic cheekbones, and the strange greenish blue of the upper eyelids.

"I wonder why Giulia never told me that so many of them were fair?" Gemma marveled aloud.

"She probably never noticed," Marco answered her. "She came to Venice with her eyes and mind tightly closed. I used to wonder why Donna Maria received her every year as neither of them enjoyed the visits much. Why did you never come in her stead?"

"I've told you," Gemma said. "Father couldn't afford for both of us to come and it was taken for granted that Nonna would prefer Giulia to me. Giulia thought she was a witch," she added inconsequentially. "She was afraid of her."

"Then why did she come? *She* knew her grandmother paid for those visits."

"Oh, no!" Gemma denied. "She came because she felt sorry for her, living in a house that's falling into the water, and which smells of dirt and damp and decay. She was right about that at least!"

"You dislike the *palazzo?*"

Gemma considered the question. "No," she said at last. "But I don't like it either. I'm rather awed by it, to tell you the truth."

"You will have time to grow used to it. Your grandmother's family have lived here for more than a thousand years. The *palazzo* was rebuilt in renaissance times, but her family were here even before that."

"As were yours?" Gemma suggested.

He shrugged. "Who knows? Perhaps mine will be here for the next thousand years."

Gemma thought he was welcome to the task of keeping the rotting framework of the palace from falling into the canal below. And yet, she couldn't deny a certain pride in knowing that these people who belonged to her grandmother's family were her family too. If she had ever doubted her Venetian inheritance, she had only to look at these portraits to know she could have sat for any one of them.

"How sad that both my uncles died," she said.

He nodded. "Your grandmother has known much tragedy in her lifetime. Remember that the next time you talk of going back to England and leaving her alone again."

"She has you."

"There is only one way she can have me. Have you seen enough of these portraits for the time being? I will show you to your room before I leave you."

Gemma jumped. She didn't want to be left alone with her grandmother, not until she had grown more used to her. "I thought you lived here," she said in a small voice.

"I do," he reassured her. "You have no need to worry that I shall desert you. I shall be back for dinner tonight."

Gemma affected indifference. "I'm afraid of getting lost in all these corridors by myself," she explained, as Marco led her through a maze of passages and rooms, each one more imposing than the last.

He turned and looked over his shoulder at her, his eyebrows raised in mockery. "Are you going to turn out to be afraid of shadows after all?"

A slanting beam of sunlight caught his face and she was overcome by the effect of the gold light on his bronzed face. She thought that she had never seen any other man whose looks could so take her breath away.

"I—why, no," she protested. "I don't think so. Though it would help if the shutters weren't kept closed all the time. One could at least see where one was going. I am glad I am not a Venetian lady. I should hate to live permanently in the shadow, no matter how pampered and perfumed the prison! All those women looked bored stiff, don't you think?"

He flung open a heavily carved door and gestured to her to precede him through it. "They had their interests," he said.

She favored him with a wide-eyed, innocent stare. "Mostly men?" she suggested. "No wonder they look bored!"

"Things have not changed in that respect. Only the very innocent could find such a topic boring, *cara*, and I doubt you are as innocent as that!"

He caught her by the hand and led her across the room to a huge window. He pushed open the shutters, securing them on great rusty hooks that had stained the wall immediately below them. He glanced at his watch, his mouth set in a cruel smile, and drew her hard up against his muscular body.

"You have the same haughty look, and are quite as vain as your ancestors, Gemma *mia*, but you are not bored by me." He bent his head, touching his lips to hers. "*That* has set your heart beating faster. The bored are not so easily flustered by the touch of a despised male."

She thought she hated him. "Go away!" she commanded him passionately. "Leave me alone!"

His hand was against her ribs and she was very conscious of it. When he removed it, he brushed against her breast and a shiver went through her that was part excitement and part fear. He flicked her nose with his forefinger, just as he might have dismissed a child.

"Do you like your room?" he asked her.

She hadn't looked at it, any more than she had looked at the busy view of the canal out of the window.

"It's very nice," she said. If he didn't go away soon and leave her alone, she would be reduced to flinging something heavy at his handsome head. She curled her hands into two fists and turned her back on him, staring out into the sunlight.

"Poor, bored little girl," he mocked her. "You have a lot to learn from those women you find so dull. They met life head on, never turning their backs on the opportunities that were presented to them. Try it and see if you don't prefer it to your safe, English ways!"

She longed to make a flashing retort to set him back on his heels, but she could think of nothing to say that wasn't childish and quite at odds with the sophisticated vision of herself she wanted to present to him. She might look like those other women, but she doubted that she would ever achieve their air of languid self-confidence. Marco made her as nervous as a cat on hot bricks.

It was a relief to hear the door shutting behind her and to be able to relax and enjoy the novelty of her surroundings. The bedroom she had been given was the most modern room she had seen in the *palazzo*. The walls had been painted in a light, indeterminate color, which she suspected may once have been some kind of pink, and the coverings on the bed were in the latest easy-care materials and had a pattern of roses spread across the *duvetyn* cover. The rugs on the floor were made from naturally colored wool in geometrical shapes of black, brown and cream.

But it was the window that drew her like a magnet,

again and again, as she unpacked her few possessions. Most of the boats were motorized now, but there were gondolas to be seen and they were as beautiful as she had always been led to believe. She forced the creaking windows open and the sounds came up to meet her as clearly as if they had been in the room with her. She tried to pick out the calls of the gondoliers from the others and once or twice she distinctly heard *premi*, meaning left, and *stali*, meaning right, but mostly it was the cry of *Oi* she heard, that could have meant anything at all.

How long she had sat at the window, she didn't know. The sunlight had turned to a golden glow, shimmering in reflection in the water, and she thought it was one of the most beautiful sights she had ever seen. More than that, it was disturbingly familiar to her, almost as if she had known it well as a child and had been away from it for a while. Perhaps, in her heart, Venice had always been her home?

A knock on her door made her turn her head. *"Avanti!"* she called out, reluctantly uncurling herself from her perch on the wide window sill.

Marco's head came round the door. "I've come to escort you to dinner. Are you ready?"

She was shocked at how much time she must have wasted. "No! Should I change? What will Nonna be wearing?"

He came right into the room, noting the dreamy look that had not yet gone from her eyes and the flush of pleasure in her cheeks. He walked over to the closet in the wall and drew out the only long dress she had with her, for she had refused to bring either of the ones

Giulia had given her. This one was far too young for her and, though it had once served its purpose when she had first started going out at night, it was far from fashionable.

"Wear this," he commanded her. He gave the garment a disparaging look. "At least it shouldn't take you long to get into it," he said. "How long have you had it?"

"Years."

His expression was inscrutable. "I think you are not as vain as your ancestors after all," he said at last. "They would not have been seen dead in such a dress!"

She snatched up the dress. "They were much older women!" she declared defiantly and disappeared into the adjoining bathroom, slamming the door behind her.

The bathroom had a quaint, Victorian air that appealed to her eye and made it seem less important that the water arrived in fits and starts, finally drying up altogether, and that the lights were so dim that she could hardly see her hand in front of her face.

Gemma was not usually nervous when she was with other people, but all the way down the stairs she tried to persuade herself that her grandmother and Marco would have so much to say to one another that she wouldn't be called upon to say anything at all.

The room where they were to dine only served to increase her nervousness. It was a room of imposing proportions, paneled from ceiling to floor in wood blackened with age and relieved only by the heraldic emblems that hung over the huge fireplace. Her grandmother was already waiting for them, seated at one end of the largest table Gemma had ever seen. She was drumming her fingers impatiently against the polished surface.

"Sit down, child, and stop looking like a frightened rabbit. We are eating down here in your honor—" She stopped, staring at her unfortunate granddaughter. "Where did you get that dress?"

Gemma's mouth set in a mutinous line. "My father never changed for dinner in his life," she said proudly.

"That I can believe," her grandmother assented. "For heaven's sake sit down, girl, and allow Marco to sit also. This table was not designed for intimate, family meals, but it is more than time that you should see the kind of life your mother was brought up to live before your father converted her to English suburbia."

"Where she was very happy," Gemma added stubbornly.

"Possibly. Giulia was very like her in some ways; you are not like her at all! You should have come to see me before."

Gemma lowered her eyes. "Giulia came every year," she pointed out.

"And became more of a stranger to me every year. Now you, my child, I understand very well indeed." She smiled her wide, ironic, faintly malicious smile. "Not only I, but Venice welcomes you. You won't escape us easily!"

"Should I want to?" Gemma asked her.

She had speedily realized that her position at the table was not the most desirable one to have. To pass anything to either of the two ends she had to half-rise out of her seat and the other two would as often as not send the required article whizzing down the other side of the table. Her grandmother sent an opened bottle of wine skidding down the table.

"Giulia would never have fitted in with my plans for the future of the *palazzo*," she said smugly. "Now you, my dear, have given me renewed hopes for the place. Don't you agree, Marco?"

Gemma's eyes went straight to his face, to be met by his dark, brooding eyes as he explored her every feature with a freedom she felt better reserved to other, more intimate circumstances.

"Marco knows I am only here for a few days at most!" she exclaimed desperately. "I have my own plans for my future and they don't include anything here in Venice. I have always known what I wanted to do. I am going to teach for a couple of years and then I am going to marry—*Freddie!*"

Her grandmother sat bolt upright, her mouth sagging at the corners like a disappointed child. "Who is this Freddie? Marco, what kind of man is he?"

The Italian spread his hands in lazy indifference. "He need not concern you, Donna Maria."

"But he does concern me! If Gemma is going back to England to be with him—"

Gemma has come to stay with you. She has a duty to you after all these years and she finds much pleasure in being with you in Venice."

"Are you sure, Marco?"

"No, he is not sure!" Gemma exploded. "He knows nothing about me!"

Marco smiled directly at her. "Nothing?"

Gemma subsided, resenting the ease with which he could disarm her. "Nothing that matters," she insisted.

Her grandmother chuckled. "How often have I

thought the same, but you will never get the better of Marco Andreotti, my child. I have never succeeded, so what hope have you?"

"I shall be going back to England!" Gemma repeated, her head held high.

The old lady's eyes snapped with amusement.

"I think not," she said. "With Giulia, Marco was unwilling, but you can learn to please him and my beloved *palazzo* will be safe for another generation. You will not be leaving Venice for a long, long time!" She stretched herself like one of the contented cats that were everywhere in the *palazzo*, coming and going at will. "You don't know how good that makes me feel, my dear, dear Gemma." She raised her glass. "You have made me very happy tonight. *Va bene, piccola*. May you be very happy also."

Chapter Five

"*Happy?* I can only be happy in England!" Gemma turned and glared at the dark man, disliking him more in that moment than she ever had before. "Freddie is a very fine person!" she said loudly.

Her grandmother's expression changed to one of stern disapproval. "As your mother found your father? Don't take that tone with me, Gemma Savage. I disapproved of your mother going out with your father and I was proved right that time. With you, I'm not going to have you throwing away your whole life on a man of the same stamp."

Gemma rose unsteadily to her feet, her eyes blinded by tears. "I won't listen to a word against Freddie. I'm going to marry him and that's that!"

The old lady sniffed. "Over my dead body!"

"If need be!" Gemma shot back at her.

Her grandmother put a hand up to her head, knocking her wig over one ear. Beneath it was revealed several long tresses of yellowing white hair. It made her seem older and more open to being hurt than Gemma liked and her exasperation and rage at being treated as if she had no mind of her own evaporated into a kind of pity.

The old lady rocked back and forth. "All that's wrong with you, young lady, is that you're afraid of a real man! However, Marco will soon change your ideas for you and you'll forget all about this Freddie of yours."

"Never!" said Gemma, her anger reviving. She turned on her heel and walked out of the room. When she gained the stairs, she was trembling. How could her grandmother, whom she had never met before that day, say such things to her? And as for Marco Andreotti! Had he known all along Donna Maria's plans for them both?

She forced her recalcitrant legs up the stairs, going she knew not where. She had to get away from them both as quickly as she could. She found herself in the gallery, faced with a row of painted ancestors looking down their noses at her.

"I'm English, do you hear me?" she addressed them fiercely. "I may look like you, but I'm not like you at all. I want to live in an English suburb and be happy as my mother was happy."

"But was she?"

Gemma's heart sank at the sound of Marco's voice. Had her mother been happy? "I don't know," she admitted.

Marco stood in the doorway, his arms folded over his chest. He looked completely at his ease and that annoyed her. Didn't he mind her grandmother pushing him into marriage with a virtual stranger?

"Should you have left Nonna on her own?" she asked him. "If she whistles for you, you won't hear her up here!"

He lifted an eyebrow. "Is that how our relationship seems to you?"

"You could have told her how it is between me and Freddie. You never said one word when she practically forced me into your arms. She must have some kind of hold on you."

"My dear girl—"

"I am not your dear anything!"

"No? Your grandmother was a little precipitate, but her instincts are sound. You will not want to teach other peoples' children for long, will you? You need a man who can set you alight and won't be afraid of being burned, not one who will despise you for having needs he can never satisfy. So, why not please your grandmother and marry me?"

"Because I've never disliked anyone as much as I dislike you!"

His smile was cruel. "That makes a good beginning. Donna Maria was afraid you would be indifferent to me, but I could have told her you were far from being that! What's the matter, Gemma? Are you remembering how you felt in my arms when I kissed you?"

"What will you get out of it?" she retorted. "The *palazzo?*"

He shook his head, taking a step toward her. "The *palazzo* is mine already."

"Then why should you want to marry me?"

"You're Donna Maria's granddaughter."

"So was Giulia! Would you have married her?"

He waved a hand in the direction of the portraits on the wall. "You are much more her granddaughter!"

"And I suppose a reflection of my grandmother is all you want in a wife!" she snapped.

"I think I can do better than that." He came another step closer. "Don't you?"

She was afraid. He was so solid and unmoveable—so aggressively male! She saw him more clearly in that instant than she had ever seen anyone before. She saw the glint in his dark eyes and knew an answering gleam of desire was reflected in her own. She lowered her lids, but she could still see every detail etched on her mind—the way his hair grew, the line of his brow, and the swift mobility of his mouth.

"I have nothing to offer you," she said.

"Nothing?"

An agitated hand rose to her face and she took a step backward.

"Shall I change your mind about disliking me, little Gemma?" Marco asked.

"No!"

"But a wife should be loving—"

"I'm not going to be your wife!"

His hands caught both hers and he drew her relentlessly closer to the hard strength of his body. She thought she would drown in the warm depths of his eyes and she tried to look away, but she could not. She licked her lips desperately, already feeling the pressure of his mouth on hers. Excitement flickered through her veins. Her whole body was tense and waiting, and *he knew it!* If she were wise, she would run away. If she were wise, she would tell him now that she wanted nothing more to do with him. If she dallied, he would never believe anything she said again. But it was more than she could do to move a muscle of her own volition.

"What a lot of fuss about nothing," he taunted her.

"It isn't nothing. I don't want to marry you!"

He sighed. "But you do want me to kiss you, don't you?"

She could not deny it. She stood there, humiliated, trying not to breathe, for every time she drew breath she could feel his hard body against her own. It was torture to be so close and yet so far away. Then he changed his grip on her hands and drew them round his back. She could feel the warmth of his chest against her breasts and her nostrils were assailed by his male smell.

"Don't you, Gemma?" he insisted softly.

"Yes!" she exploded.

It was bliss to feel his hands against her back and to be brought up hard against him, lifting her almost off her feet as his mouth descended on hers, parting her lips with a calm detachment she wished she could imitate. She felt his tongue against hers and uttered a meaningless sound.

When he put her away from him, her knees threatened to give way and she clung to him, afraid she would fall. The bodice of her dress, never very secure for she had had it from the days before she was fully grown, had come apart and the curve of her breasts was clearly revealed to him. He spread his hands over the two globes and kissed her again, more gently, first on the mouth and then on her tightly shut eyes.

"Do you dislike me now?" he asked her.

She could not answer. How did she know how she felt about him when he could arouse her as he was doing now? This man had destroyed her defenses as easily as if they had been made of straw. How was it that he had only to touch her for her to melt into his arms?

"I—you—it isn't *right!*" she exclaimed. "You have no right—"

"But you have such a beautiful body," he said in her ear.

"That's no excuse for—" she broke off, her cheeks scarlet, as his fingers found and caressed her nipple— *"that!"* she concluded on a gasp. "Marco?"

"When did I first call you beautiful?"

"When you first saw me." *She remembered it all too well!* "You said, '*Buona sera, bellissima signorina,*' but you didn't mean it, any more than you mean it now!"

He smiled. "How do you know that?"

"I can tell. You'd dally with any female who crossed your path. Only, why with me?"

"Because when I marry I want a woman in my arms. Even if you don't like me, Gemma Savage, you want me as much as I want you. Whatever else it is, it won't be dull married to you."

She would like to have denied that she felt anything for him at all, but she knew he would never believe her. He probably knew exactly how she was feeling; he probably even knew that no other man had ever stirred her blood, taken her lips as if by right with his own, or had handled her body with a freedom she could not deny him.

"I hate you!" she burst out.

His eyes caught fire. "Do you? Do you, Gemma *mia?* Then why don't you cover yourself from my gaze? I'm not holding you now."

The material would barely meet across her swollen breasts, and *he* had done this to her! She could have cried with frustration and a curious, sinking disappointment that he had not gone on kissing her.

She took the only refuge that was open to her and burst into tears. She covered her face with her hands and turned her back on him. But she might have known that it would take more than a few feminine tears to defeat him.

"What do you want, Gemma? For me to kiss you, or leave you alone?"

She gave him a look that would have withered a lesser man where he stood. "You know what I want. I want to marry Freddie."

"You didn't last night in London," he reminded her. "You were on the brink of discovering you were bored silly with him—"

"He's *nice*. *He* doesn't—" But it proved impossible to tell Marco what Freddie didn't do. He had never undressed her with his eyes for a start, nor had he ever come so near doing so in actual fact as Marco had done. She shivered, remembering the feel of his hands on her flesh.

"If he marries you," Marco continued grimly, "it will be too late for you to find out that he holds as much interest for you as yesterday's porridge. Grow up, Gemma, and think about somebody else for a change. It cost your grandmother a great deal to send for you when you've never come near her all these years. She's not a rich woman these days, but she's willing to share what she has with you; what will you do for her? Why don't you do as she wants and marry me?"

Gemma stopped crying, shocked by the very idea. "Because I don't love you and you don't love me!" she wailed.

"And you think you do love Freddie?" he mocked her.

"I do! You don't know anything about it!" she claimed. "I admit I was a bit impatient with him last night, but it didn't mean anything. I've known him forever. I feel *safe* with him, if you want to know. You wouldn't understand!"

"No, I wouldn't," he agreed. He put a hand under her chin and turned her face to his. "Foolish Gemma, it's you who doesn't understand. You may want to be prim and proper and all that is virtuous, but you never will be as far as I'm concerned. You need a man to love you, *piccina mia*, not some fumbling lover who'll reduce you to frustration and make you contemptuous of everything he does."

Gemma's mouth trembled. The relentless pressure of his fingers on her chin was sufficiently disturbing to make it very difficult to think straight.

"The only difference is that you're more experienced!" she declared bravely.

Marco made a sound with his tongue. "Come down from the clouds, Gemma, and learn a little honesty." His lips brushed hers and, against her will, she arched her body against him, her resolutions of never allowing herself to be touched by him again all forgotten. He stepped away from her, his face set and unyielding. He put his cheek against hers, not holding her at all, but keeping her there against him by sheer force of will. "If I were to invite you into my bed, could you refuse me, little Gemma?"

She gasped and tried to push him away, but his mouth covered hers again and her fingers clung to him, holding him closer against her.

"I thought not," he murmured.

Gemma hugged herself defensively, refusing to answer. She felt as though she had never known herself at all. How could she be so—so *wanton* as to long to fling herself into this man's arms, regardless of whether he loved her or not, merely to indulge herself in that sudden ecstasy that he seemed to be able to induce in her at will? There was more to marriage than a flaring of desire, destined to burn out as quickly as the fireworks it so much resembled in her blood. Marriage was growing old together and fusing shared interests. She sighed. With Marco she would never be certain he was not with another woman, forgetting all about her! He didn't love her and, once he had what he wanted from her—but what did he want? Was all this only to please the old woman who had been kind to him when he was a child? Gemma didn't understand him at all.

The door opened and her grandmother came in, leaning heavily on the two sticks she always had with her. She looked from one to the other of them, but she said nothing. A gray cat emerged from under her skirts and wound itself round her leg in a movement of affection.

"Cats," she muttered with a tolerant shrug of her shoulders. "Ah well, Venice would not be Venice without them."

"Who feeds them all?" Gemma asked.

Her grandmother's shrewd eyes rested briefly on her face, traveled down to her scarcely buttoned bodice and back again. Gemma blushed. Was it very obvious she had just been kissed? She hoped not. With all her heart, she hoped not!

"Everyone feeds them," the old lady said. "Not very well, but they are not like other cats. Venetian cats don't live solitary lives, waiting for handouts from their human owners. They congregate in gangs and live a social life of their own. We must have hundreds of them, coming and going, here in the *palazzo,* but none of them really belongs to us."

"Oh," said Gemma. "Giulia never mentioned the cats. She never told us anything interesting about Venice—"

"Venice didn't interest her, that's why. You should have come in her stead, Gemma, and seen Venice for yourself."

"But there wasn't enough money for the two of us to come!"

"I would have found the money, child. I've found the money for you to come now, haven't I?"

Gemma chewed on her lower lip. "I thought my father paid for Giulia to come," she said at last. "I didn't know it was you. I'm sorry, Nonna, I didn't think to thank you now either. It was all such a rush I never thought about who had paid for my ticket. I won't be able to pay you back until the end of the term."

"Marco will see to it!"

"No!" That, she knew, she could not allow. That would be the last straw! "I'll manage. Only, I don't know how soon I can pay you back."

"Forget it, my dear," her grandmother advised her.

"I would have paid for you to come and see me a long time ago if I'd thought you'd come. Didn't Giulia ever tell you that?"

Gemma shook her head, her eyes bright with tears. If she could have come when she had been younger, she would have come to love her grandmother long ago. There was no denying the link between them, which was more than merely looking alike on the outside, they were alike on the inside too, two of a kind—and they both loved Marco Andreotti!

The blood rushed from her head and she thought she might faint. It couldn't be true! Of course it wasn't! But how else could she account for the fact that he had only to lift his little finger for her to fall into his arms?

She pulled her attention back to what her grandmother was saying, a slightly bemused expression on her face.

"The first thing is to get you some clothes, my dear. That dress you're wearing is scarcely decent. You look as though you're about to pop out of it at any moment. And your day dresses are not much better."

Gemma opened her eyes wide. "But, Nonna, I can't possibly afford a whole new wardrobe just now. I have clothes, really I have. They're not very smart perhaps, but they're quite good enough for school and they're very comfortable."

Marco shook his head at her. "You need something other than a tweed skirt and a shapeless cardigan in Venice," he advised her. "We can't have you mistaken for a tourist."

Her grandmother smiled a wintry smile. "Is that possible with her looks?" she asked.

"But I am a tourist, Nonna!" Gemma cried out.

"Rubbish, girl. My granddaughter is not a tourist in my own city. She is one of us, and she must look the part. If I am not well enough to take you shopping tomorrow, Marco will have to do it, but clothes you must have."

"Italian clothes are so expensive," Gemma sighed helplessly.

"Good things generally are, but that is my worry, my dear." She put out a thin, bony hand, that was somehow still elegant in movement. "It was as much my fault as yours that you didn't come to see me sooner and this is my opportunity for making it up to you. I am proud to have a truly Venetian granddaughter at last and this is my way of saying so."

Gemma was touched. "Thank you, Nonna," she said meekly. She looked up in time to see the mocking expression on Marco's face. "But I won't go shopping with him!" she declared, jerking her chin in his direction.

Her grandmother looked amused. "He would make you a better advisor than an old woman who has scarcely left the *palazzo* in years."

"I don't doubt it, if I wanted to dress like a woman of the world," Gemma retorted, "but he knows nothing about your granddaughter. He never will!"

"I wonder." The old lady passed off the remark as if it were of no particular interest. "It's been a long day," she said, a twinkle in her eyes. "Marco, will you see me to my room?" The Contessa's smile was easy and affectionate, as Marco eased her up onto her feet.

"Good night, Nonna," Gemma said rather awkwardly, not wanting to go anywhere near Marco and defeated by the stick her grandmother was wielding on the other side.

"Aren't you going to kiss me good night?" her grandmother asked ironically.

"Yes. Yes, of course. Good night, Nonna," Gemma said again, planting a fleeting kiss on the wrinkled, perfumed cheek.

"My dear child, is that the best you can do?" Her grandmother's expression changed to one of knowing sympathy. "Is it because I'm old? I remember when I was young I hated to touch very old people. I thought they smelled of old age, a clinging, sweet smell that never went away. Somehow one never thinks of oneself as being old like that."

"But you're not!" Gemma protested. "I love you dearly. But your stick's in my way and—"

Her grandmother laughed out loud. "Marco won't eat you."

"I didn't think he would," Gemma denied, more flustered than ever.

"I'm asking you to kiss *me* good night, not him," the old lady went on, plainly enjoying herself. "He can look after himself." She gently poked him in the ribs, smiling at him. "If he hasn't done so already?" Gemma didn't dare look at him. She took a quick step toward her grandmother, embracing her fondly and putting her face willingly against hers.

"Thank you for bringing me here, Nonna," she said.

Marco's hand came down on her shoulder. "I'll take Donna Maria to her room and then, perhaps, you'd like to go out?"

She shook her head wildly. "Not tonight. I think I'll follow Nonna's example and go to bed."

If she could find her room! She knew by the glint in his eyes that the thought had occurred to him also. If it took her all night, she would find her bedroom by herself. She didn't need his help—for anything!

"Good night, Marco," she said defiantly, as her grandmother painfully negotiated her way through the door before him.

He turned and looked at her, and her brief triumph crumbled to dust.

"Good night, Gemma *mia*," he said.

Chapter Six

"You look very nice," the Contessa congratulated Gemma, "and *very* Venetian!"

Gemma was also pleased with the results of their shopping. She had never had so many new clothes all at once, never in her whole life, nor had she ever had the opportunity to take only those which really suited her, enhancing her coloring and giving her a new elegance that did a tremendous amount for her confidence.

"Nonna, I shall owe you so much money," she had protested at intervals, but her grandmother had paid no attention to such fainthearted objections.

"Marco is used to his women being well-dressed—and well-mannered too," her grandmother retorted.

"He expects too much!" Gemma said sharply.

"Most men do," Donna Maria agreed humorously.

She looked extremely tired, but happy to have accomplished such a change in her granddaughter's appearance in such a short time.

"My dear, you are more Venetian than English," she commented proudly.

"I've been an ordinary English girl all my life!" Gemma insisted.

Her grandmother's eyes were kind, even a little sad. "But you never will be again. You may pretend to be as English as your father was, but you are your mother's daughter, and my granddaughter."

There was no denying that. Gemma had found it quite embarrassing to listen to the comments about herself that had been made to her grandmother in all the shops they had visited. Wherever they had gone, the same excited whispers had met them, and the same compliments had been paid to the Contessa on the Venetian looks of her new granddaughter which were so like the Contessa's own.

She looked at her grandmother now, noting the lines of pain that showed on her face and the dark blotches of fatigue round her eyes. She hoped it hadn't been too much for her, traipsing about Venice in and out of her private gondola with never a word of complaint. There was a bravery about the old lady that struck a chord in Gemma's heart. Even that ridiculous wig she insisted on wearing was no more than a defiant gesture against the arthritis which had crippled her joints and the aging process she so evidently hated in herself.

"I hope it wasn't too much for you coming shopping with me?" Gemma worried over her.

"Of course not," the older woman denied. "And if it was, what am I saving myself for, I'd like to know?"

Gemma put her hand on hers. "You're being very kind to me, Nonna, I wish there was something I could do for you?"

"You could marry Marco."

Gemma bit her lip. "No, not that! I don't like him very much. Oh, I know he's been very kind to you, but he despises me."

"Despises you? My dear girl, why ever should he do that?"

"He thinks I neglected you. He doesn't understand that we always thought Giulia's visits would give you more pleasure because she *looked* so Italian. And we were always told that only one of us could go."

The old lady sighed. "Your father had little sympathy with foreigners. It was unfortunate he should have fallen in love with one. He wanted your mother enough to marry her, but he never forgave her for not being English, not even after her death. Poor man, it can't have been easy for him, raising two little girls on his own, but all my offers to have you with me were rejected out of hand. I think he knew that once I'd seen you, I'd never let you go again! He must have known how like me you are, and he, too, had seen the portraits up in the gallery when he was courting your mother. I can imagine how he felt when you turned out to be a replica of me—the woman he most disliked."

"But he couldn't have disliked you," Gemma protested.

"Why not? He didn't see me with your eyes, *cara*. He saw me as the embodiment of everything he most disliked. I speak English with an accent and I expect to be treated in a certain way for no better reason than because I live in a *palazzo* and can trace my family line back several generations farther than he could. Worst of all, I was against his marrying my daughter. He accused me of not thinking him good enough for her—and he was quite right, I didn't. I knew he wouldn't love her enough. But she was not like you and I, I think. We need men who will ask much of us and give as much in return. Is it not so?"

Gemma was embarrassed. "I've never thought about it," she admitted.

"No, but now you have me to think about it for you. I mean to be a better grandmother to you than I was a mother to your mother. This time there will be no mistake and you will live happily ever after."

Gemma managed a small, reluctant smile. "With Freddie?" she suggested.

But to her surprise her grandmother only smiled back at her. "Maybe, if this Freddie is the right man for you."

"I thought only Marco could possibly be that?" Gemma commented wryly.

Her grandmother's face softened. "Marco is very special to me. I should be happy if he were to be special to you too, but I am old enough to know that if there is no spark between a man and a woman it's better for them to go their separate ways. If you feel nothing for Marco, I am still your grandmother, my dear. I won't pretend I won't be disappointed, but I may come to like your Freddie just as much as you think I will." She closed her mouth with a little snap, bringing the conversation firmly to an end. "I think I will go and have a rest now after our busy morning. What will you do with yourself?"

"I thought I'd go sightseeing," she said. "I have a

guidebook I bought at the airport. I thought I might take a look at the Doges' Palace, unless you'd rather I stayed in with you?"

"No, no, my dear. You'd soon get bored if you were to do nothing but attend to me. See me up to my room, if you will, but then I can manage quite well on my own."

It was a long process getting her grandmother up the stairs and it tore at Gemma's heart to see how crippled she was. She was of an age to suffer from arthritis of course, but living in the permanently damp *palazzo* could hardly help her.

"Shall I help you undress?" she offered as they finally reached her grandmother's bedroom door.

"You spoil me as much as Marco does," the old lady chided her. "He thinks I can't lift hand or foot for myself. Would it be too much bother, my dear?"

"It would be a pleasure," Gemma insisted. "I think I'm the one who is being spoiled. I've never had so many new things before, and each one lovelier than the last. I can never thank you enough, Nonna, and especially for coming with me."

"It was more fun than I've had for a long, long time. You're looking very nice now, very *chic*, Marco will be pleased."

"It's whether you're pleased that I care about.' Gemma insisted.

"I am, child. Go out and enjoy yourself now and don't hurry home. We never eat before eight o'clock in the evening and I doubt if I shall get up again before then. Have a good time and keep away from all the young men. They can be very persistent when they spot a pretty young girl on her own."

Gemma couldn't resist taking a long, cool look at herself in the glass in her own room before she went out again. It was only the clothes, she thought, but there seemed to be a new light in her eyes and a new, softer line to her mouth. Such elegance could never have been acquired in the sort of shops she usually patronized, but then nobody of her acquaintance bought their shoes at Zecchi's, their dresses from Ma Boutique in the *calle* Larga San Marco, nor did they have their hair done at hideous expense at a place called Carol's, where her grandmother sent her wigs to be washed. No wonder she felt a trifle like Cinderella—and she knew who would prick the balloon of her conceit when he saw her, turning her clothes back to rags. Marco Andreotti would know she was exactly the same person underneath as she had always been, whose only interest for him was that she was her grandmother's granddaughter.

She took a *vaporetto* to the Doges' Palace. The strange odor of the canals assailed her nostrils as she settled herself in her seat beside a matron of ample proportions who was returning home with her shopping.

Gemma mentioned that she was getting out at the Doges' Palace. "Will you tell me when we get there?" she asked her neighbor.

The woman said she had never been so far away from home in her life, but there would be others who would see that she got out at the right stop. She proceeded to announce to everyone in the boat where Gemma was going, adding that she wouldn't have believed she was English to look at her, that she looked like a true Venetian.

"My mother came from Venice," Gemma told her.

All the passengers of the *vaporetto* turned and stared at her, admiring her good sense at being half a Venetian at least. Her neighbor shrugged, her face wreathed in a smile. "It's better than being an Italian," she said. "I have never wanted to be one of them."

Gemma was amused. "Isn't Venice in Italy?" she inquired.

"Venice is Venice, *signorina*. Why should it want to be anything else?"

Gemma was sorry to lose her new friends when they hurried her ashore by the imposing edifice that turned out to be the Doges' Palace, all of them wishing her a happy afternoon, laughing and waving at her as if they had know her all her life.

She felt truly happy as she turned away. She felt at home in Venice, despite her limping Italian, and she was glad the people seemed to like her as much as she liked them. Not for the first time, she wished she had known her mother, to know if she had been a Venetian at heart, but she suspected that, like Giulia, her mother would not have known what she was talking about. How could she have left all this behind her? How would Gemma be able to leave it when the time came for her to go home?

Resolutely, she put all such thoughts out of her head and concentrated on the impressive magnificence of the palace she had come to see. Her guidebook advised her that the lower arcade was called the *broglio*. It was here the merchants and politicians of old had walked and talked and had become involved in the occasional imbroglio, many of them ugly incidents that had led to death or long imprisonment. Gemma walked in their wake, glad she was alive now rather than then. In those days a woman needed a strong protector if she were to survive the family feuds and quarrels that surrounded her. Someone like Marco, who would smooth her path and keep the predators away.

Marco again! It was almost as if he were the spirit of Venice. If only she could think about him without that shiver of excitement spreading through her body. Marco might be offering her marriage—though only to please her grandmother—but he wasn't offering her security. Gemma thought she knew exactly what marriage to him would be like.

She forced her attention back to her surroundings and the arcade along which she was walking. Staring up at the carvings above the capitals she found she could also see out into the courtyard. Marco was standing there. She thought he was a figment of her imagination and blinked, half-hoping he would vanish in a cloud of smoke. He was still there, however, when she opened her eyes again, standing in that arrogant way of his, with his arms crossed in front of his chest, as if the whole world had been created for his exclusive use. Gemma's heart missed a beat. He was undeniably handsome, powerful looking and aggressively male. It made her feel weak and feminine just to look at him. The memory of his kisses haunted her, waking and sleeping, and one look from those dark, gleaming eyes of his was enough to turn her bones to jelly and arouse some need within herself that scared her half to death.

Then, even as she watched, a young woman came running across the courtyard, flinging herself into Marco's outstretched arms, and he bent his head and kissed her right on the mouth. It was Gisela.

Gemma dropped her guidebook and found she was trembling as she stooped to pick it up. Gisela was beautiful and it was no wonder she had caught Marco's eye. Gemma felt a sharp pain in her breast as she saw the warm, affectionate smile with which Marco greeted her, holding both her hands in his, and obviously inquiring anxiously after her welfare.

Gemma abandoned her sightseeing and stepped out into the courtyard herself. She had forgotten her new clothes, forgotten everything in her determination to attract Marco's attention, though why she should want to, when she didn't even like him, she never paused to consider.

"Marco!" she called out.

His shoulders stiffened as he turned to face her, his eyes traveling up and down her with a proprietary air that she hated. The color came flooding up into her face, but she refused to droop her head, or show him in any other way that she resented his treatment of her. On the contrary, she raised defiant eyes to his and gave him back look for look.

"What are you doing here?" he asked her.

"I'm here. Isn't that good enough for you?" she retorted.

"Following me?" he suggested, his voice as smooth as silk.

She shrugged her shoulders. "Venice isn't your private property."

"I don't care for being spied on, Gemma *mia*. What I do in my own time, away from the *palazzo*, is my own business, not yours. Is that clear?"

"I might say the same to you," she answered, stung by his attitude. "I have a right to my privacy too."

"You have no such rights. What young girl has? Does your grandmother know you're here?"

"What if she doesn't?"

"I'd think you even more selfish than I do already. She is old and tired and, by the look of you, she has already given you a great deal of her time and energy today. If you give her any trouble, Gemma Savage, you'll have me to answer to!"

"Nonna sent me out to have a look at Venice," Gemma told him in such even tones that he should have been warned she was about to lose her temper.

"By yourself? Our Venetian men are not like Englishmen. You'll be lucky if you return to the *palazzo* with only a few bruises to show for your adventure!"

"It's better than being mentally undressed as you do every time you look at me!" Gemma flared.

He laughed, throwing back his head, and said something Gemma didn't catch in Italian to Gisela, and the Italian girl began to laugh too.

"Those clothes are hardly designed to hide your attractions underneath," he observed. "If you want men to ignore you, you'd best go back to your skirts and shapeless cardigans."

"I dress to please myself!" she claimed.

She was thrown off balance by Gisela's unexpectedly sweet smile. The Italian girl put an arm round her shoulders and hugged her close.

"You mustn't mind Marco," she said in Italian, her voice low and husky. "He doesn't mean to be unkind. Were you visiting the Doges' Palace?"

Gemma nodded. Was this girl so sure of Marco that she didn't mind Gemma's abrupt entry into their meeting?

"We went shopping this morning, but this afternoon my grandmother was tired and suggested I should see something of Venice—"

"You are looking lovely," Gisela congratulated her. "I scarcely recognized you at first. I saw you before once. I was standing on a bridge when you and Marco passed underneath. But now you look truly Venetian yourself! Marco, you haven't said how well she is looking."

Marco looked her up and down once more. "Very nice. Your grandmother has good taste."

Gemma glared at him. "I choose my own clothes!"

She would like to have included Gisela in her anger, but the Italian girl was so obviously nice that this was proving very difficult.

"The shoes are from Zecci," Gemma murmured.

"As one can see," Gisela nodded. "You are fortunate to have such pretty legs. They look lovely in good shoes. Most Italians are rather short in the leg, but you have the best of both worlds."

"I'm not used to such high heels," Gemma confessed. "I nearly didn't wear them this afternoon as I was going sightseeing, but they are much more comfortable than I thought they would be. They fit exactly."

"Shoes are meant to fit exactly," Gisela protested.

"But they more often fit where they touch," Gemma smiled. "At least mine do."

"Not Venetian shoes!"

They laughed together comfortably, as if they had known each other for a long, long time.

"I am sure Gemma would like to join us for a coffee in the Piazza," Gisela said to Marco, brushing a hair off the lapel of his coat. "Now, now, we will have no dark looks. People are used to seeing you with one pretty woman hanging on your arm, imagine what they will think when they see two of us! We look good together, no?"

Marco smiled reluctantly. "You must speak slowly, Gisela, if you want Gemma to understand you. She is only learning Italian—"

"It will get better. I don't speak English at all, so it will have to get better." She pulled his arm about her shoulders with the assurance of one who has never been rejected. "She is nice, this Gemma of yours, and you are not to frighten her away, Marco. I know what you Andreottis are like! You have your pick of all the women and that is how you behave. Try a little gentleness, believe me, it will work very well for you."

He hugged her to him. "Gemma likes to pretend she is engaged to an Englishman," he told her. "His name is Freddie."

But Gisela only laughed. "And what does the Contessa say to that? Come, let us go and have some coffee. Quadri's? Or Florian's?" she asked Gemma, mentioning the two most famous cafes in Venice.

"We will go to Florian's," Marco answered for her. "Gemma is a romantic. She will like to think of Wagner sitting in the same place where she is sitting and complaining that no one applauds his music."

"I prefer to think of Proust correcting the proofs of his translation of Ruskin," Gemma said coldly.

"They were all tourists," Gisela sighed, "but at least we don't look like tourists, not even you, Gemma."

"Gemma least of all," Marco said dryly. He watched her flushed face with thoughtful eyes. "I don't think she has ever been a tourist before. She never said anything, but flying to Venice was her first flight, wasn't it, Gemma?"

"What if it were?"

Gisela slapped the table sharply with her open hand. "You must not mind Marco. He wishes you had come before, instead of that sister of yours, but he can't bring himself to say so." She pulled a quick face at the man opposite her. "Gemma probably knows you didn't like Giulia so there's no need to look like that."

"I know Giulia didn't like him," Gemma put in. It gave her pleasure to think how much her sister had disliked him. She had never had anything nice to say about the "horrid boy" who had lived at the poor end of the street.

"It may be well to remember that Gemma is her sister," Marco said to Gisela.

Gisela nodded her head in her forthright way. "But still. . . . Do you remember how Giulia would never speak to me?"

"I do," Marco agreed grimly.

"Yet Gemma is as easy to talk to as one of my own friends. She doesn't think herself any better than I am, do you, Gemma?"

Gemma looked puzzled. "I like you very much," she said.

Marco put his cup down with a clatter. "I wonder why?" He glanced at his watch. "It's time you were going, Gemma *mia*. You came to Venice to be with your grandmother, not to be with us. Come, and I will see you into the right *vaporetto* to take you home. Say good-bye to Gisela."

"But—" Gemma began in English.

"You have interrupted us for long enough," he cut her off in the same language. "Gisela has something she wishes to say to me in private and I won't have you taking advantage of her good manners."

To Gemma's dismay the tears welled up in her eyes and she averted her face quickly in case he should see them.

"I didn't realize I was intruding," she said proudly.

"You do now. Go back to your grandmother, Gemma, and wait for me to make the running. You have much to learn as to how a Venetian lady behaves and I do not enjoy being followed by you round the city."

Gemma said good-bye to Gisela in perfect Italian, but the light had gone out of her eyes. Gisela looked from one to the other of them, a puzzled expression on her face. "Must you truly go?" she asked Gemma.

"Yes. I hope I shall see you again sometime?"

"Of course." Gisela looked more puzzled than ever. "Marco will give you my address."

But Gemma would never ask him for it, on that she was determined. "There is no need for you to come with me," she said as he rose to go with her. "I prefer to go alone."

Gemma sat in a frozen silence as the *vaporetto* transported her home. She was hurt, but even more she was angry. How dare he speak to her like that? She stepped out of the *vaporetto* and ran along the short *calle* to her grandmother's home. The door was standing open and she went straight inside and up the stairs to the small sitting room where her grandmother was waiting for her.

"What is the matter, child?" Donna Maria asked. taking one look at her face.

"I wouldn't marry him if he were the last man on earth!" Gemma stormed at her. "He has a very odd idea of what any wife will put up with!" She took a deep breath, disturbed by the sheer agony she felt in her heart. "He's in love with somebody else. Nonna, who *is* Gisela?"

Chapter Seven

"Who is Gisela?" Gemma repeated.

"Gisela? Just Gisela? How should I know?"

"But you must know her, Nonna. Marco obviously knows her very well indeed, and she knew Giulia too."

The old lady smiled serenely. "I cannot remember that Marco has ever introduced her to me."

"Doesn't he bring any of his friends here? I've seen her before today. She was standing on one of the bridges over the canal when Marco brought me to the *palazzo*. He was very odd about her then. I think he's in love with her!"

"Very likely!"

Gemma stared at her grandmother in dismay. "Nonna, how can you say so?"

Her grandmother shrugged. "What business is it of

mine? Or yours either? Marco is very much a man. Women are necessary to him and it is best not to inquire too closely into what he does when he is not at home. It's the way of men. Even my own dear husband, who was goodness itself to me, heaven knows, couldn't resist a pretty face when he saw one. One has to accept these things, my dear."

"Why?" Gemma perched herself on the arm of her grandmother's chair, swinging one leg back and forth from the knee in her agitation. "Why should I accept any such thing?"

"Most wives do."

"Not English wives!" Gemma claimed, wondering even as she did so as to the truth of that. "*I* won't! Nonna, how can you want me to marry a Lothario who'll never be content with one woman—not even one woman at a time? And I daresay he's one of the worst when it comes to insisting on having a virtuous wife. It's outrageous!"

"My dear child, are you going to change the world single-handedly? The female sex has always been the more realistic, especially when it comes to the failings of others. You will be the same. We all go through an idealistic period when we first fall in love, thinking that we will be different, that the men we love are going to be different, but as often as not we find we are just the same as everyone else, and so are they. Be thankful that Marco will keep all such affairs away from you and his family and that you needn't know a thing about it if you don't want to. And why should one want to? What good does it do?"

Gemma was silent though she had never met this Italian attitude to marriage before and she found it quite shocking that it should be taken for granted that men should be unfaithful to their wives, but never wives to their husbands.

"*Cara*, if you're going to sit and fume and say nothing, please find your own chair to sit on. I find sewing a fine seam awkward enough these days without you rocking my arm like that!"

Gemma apologized abstractedly. Her grandmother continued her lecture. "To live with a man is not like having a pleasant brother in the house with you."

"Of course not!" But it was hard to imagine what it would be like living with someone like Marco Andreotti. One would have no say in anything. But would it be worth it to have a man like that for a husband? The heat in her cheeks embarrassed her as much as her own thoughts.

It was an odd kind of conversation to be having with one's grandmother, but the Contessa was far easier to talk to than even Giulia had been. It was a novel experience for her to have someone of her own to whom she could say what she liked. Her grandmother might be old, but she had not forgotten what it was like to be a woman.

"My dear, the time to object is when no man looks at you. To attract the eye of a man like Marco is better than being ignored by him, surely?"

"I'm not sure. He's so *physical!*"

"And you're not?"

Her grandmother's needle didn't pause. She was embroidering a new silk nightdress for Gemma, as she had always embroidered her own when she had been young. Gemma thought it far too beautiful to wear, but Donna Maria had ignored this comment as being beneath her notice. One day she might be glad of it, she had remarked.

"What does this Freddie mean to you, Gemma?" she asked now. "Is it really true that you want to marry him?"

"I think so. I've known him for ages."

"And your father approved of him?"

"He didn't disapprove."

The Contessa's eyes glinted with suppressed amusement. "Not even when he caught him kissing you in the garden shed?"

Gemma frowned. "Freddie isn't the kind of person anyone would disapprove of," she tried to explain. "Giulia thought him dull, but even she thought him a suitable husband for me."

"How exciting!" her grandmother interjected.

"But I don't like excitement!" Gemma exclaimed. "Most people would think Marco was exciting, but I don't. He's arrogant and dangerous, and I'd never be able to call my soul my own, and not even you would expect him to be faithful to me, not even when we were first married. What's so exciting about that?"

Donna Maria's eyebrows rose. "It would be a challenge for you to keep him at home, *cara*. Now you have the proper clothes you are a very beautiful young woman. Wouldn't you care to try to tame Marco and see if you couldn't make him love only you? You ought to have more confidence in yourself. You give the impression of being scared of your own shadow."

"Giulia—"

Her grandmother suddenly looked cross. "Don't always be comparing yourself to your sister, Gemma! She would never have been half the woman you will be!

She was pretty enough, but you will be beautiful even when you are as old as I am. She was an ordinary little suburban soul who wanted nothing more than a labor-saving apartment and a labor-saving husband; you look as much at home in the *palazzo* as if you'd been born and raised here and, sooner or later, you will want more from your husband than the latest washing machine."

Gemma stared at her. "I always thought of Giulia as being someone special. She *was* someone special! She came to see you every summer—"

"My dear child, that was no treat for either of us. In her heart, she never left your father's home. She disliked me, and she disliked Venice too. Be honest now. Won't you miss Venice when you go back to London?"

Gemma would have preferred not to have answered. She was in love with Venice, she thought. Giulia had told her about the decaying splendor, but she had made it sound as though it were somehow horrible, like mushrooms growing on rotten wood in the cellar. She had stressed the smell of the canals, saying it made her feel sick as often as not. And she had described their grandmother as a witch, when she was in reality a fading beauty who resented growing old and was putting up a gallant last-ditch struggle against the ravages of age. But Giulia had been wrong! Gemma wouldn't have changed anything, not even the duck-boards assuring one of dry feet in the famous Piazza of San Marco.

"I can always come back," she said.

"With Freddie?"

But Freddie wouldn't like Venice any more than

Giulia had! "Freddie will understand that I shall want to come and see you—often." Gemma tried to convince herself as much as her grandmother.

"I wonder." Donna Maria held the nightdress up in front of her, admiring her own handiwork. "Why don't you invite him to visit you here? If you're going to marry him, it's only fair he should know the Venetian side of your nature."

"He's always known my mother was an Italian."

"Your mother, yes, but does he know you're as much one of us as you are English. I don't suppose that was particularly obvious when you were in England, have you thought of that?"

"I'm the same person now I've always been," Gemma said.

Her grandmother laughed. "Right now you don't look English at all, my love. Even your Italian is far more fluent than it was yesterday. If your father could see you now, I'm afraid all his worst fears would be realized. He wouldn't have enjoyed having a beautiful, Venetian young lady for a daughter. To think it was Guilia he worried about!"

Gemma gave her an uncomfortable look. "Father treated us both the same always."

"I'm sure." The gentle mockery disturbed Gemma as nothing that had gone before had done. Her father had preferred Giulia, she had always known that, but he had never denied his younger daughter her due. Of that she was certain. Well, she was almost certain.

"I wonder if Freddie would come," she mused aloud.

"Why not, if you are important to him? If you're worried that I won't be civil to him, you need not. I have had years and years in which to learn how to behave toward guests of all sorts in my home."

Gemma smiled. "Nonna, I love you!" she exclaimed.

"I look forward to meeting your Freddie," Donna Maria said carefully. She folded up the nightdress she was embroidering and smiled at her granddaughter. "The sooner you invite him to join you, the sooner he'll come. I'll enclose a note of my own to go in with yours. Shall I go and write it now?"

Gemma thanked her. She was undecided as to what she would say to Freddie herself. Supposing he were to let her down and not come after all? Supposing he didn't like her enough to want to come? And if he came, what would Marco think of him? She found to her dismay that she was shaking. Marco, Marco, always Marco! What was the matter with her that she could think of nothing else but Marco? But she could not. Try as she would, all she could think was how nice it would be to have someone presentable to dangle in front of Marco's eyes as he had dangled Gisela in front of hers! How small-minded, she castigated herself, but she didn't care. Somehow she had to show Marco that the physical attraction between them was nothing more than that, that she didn't like him, and couldn't admire the way he treated her or any other woman.

Did she want to be dominated by a man who thought nothing of her? Did she want to be made use of as Marco had made use of her, bending her to his will as though men were born to command and women to serve? Was that what she wanted?

Her heart beat frantically against her ribs as she remembered how, while she had been shamed by his easy conquest, her body had welcomed him with an enthusiasm she now wanted to deny. How many other women felt the same way about him? How many were there who thought themselves to be in love with Marco Andreotti?

She made herself go to her room and penned a letter to Freddie, inviting him to Venice. She read it through and thought how distant and unwelcoming it sounded, almost as if she didn't really want him to come at all. But it would have to do. She put her letter in an envelope and addressed it, frowning over the task because she still had to persuade herself that she really wanted to send it. Her grandmother's note came with one of the maids, a young girl Gemma hadn't seen before.

"You will want a stamp, *signorina*. Shall I take it to the post for you?"

"Is it far?" Gemma asked her.

"No, there is a tobacconist at the end of the *calle*. You may buy a stamp there, and cards also, anything the *signorina* may need in the way of stationery."

Gemma put her grandmother's letter with her own and stuck down the envelope with an air of resignation. It was still the middle of the term, she remembered, and Freddie was unlikely to miss any days when he should have been at work. Perhaps he wouldn't come after all.

She had not been down the *calle* before. It meant going out of the back door of the *palazzo*, which stood open all day long, a barred gate keeping the unwanted intruder from coming in. There was some difficulty in finding the key and the gate creaked from lack of use when Gemma finally forced it open. She left it on the latch and ran down the *calle*, her letter in her hand.

The smell of the *calle* was even worse than that of the canal. Some children, their clothes in rags and the grime of many days obscuring the fairness of their features, were playing a complicated game of ball against a tenement wall. Gemma paused to watch them, wondering if Marco had played the same game there when he had been their age. Marco again! She could have wept to have caught herself thinking of him again. Had she no pride at all?

It was getting late. The light had changed to its evening glow of pure gold, lending the whole city a romantic disguise. Gemma walked across the marble floor and went to stand by the main doors where she could see down the whole length of the canal.

She leaned against the jamb of the door, her hands behind her back, and half closed her eyes for the light from the sun was almost too bright for her.

The scene she had been watching stuck in her mind's eye and she was overcome by its beauty. Water and light were always a fascinating combination and to have it outside one's own front door was luxury indeed.

She opened her eyes again and there was Marco, looking at her with an amused expression in his dark eyes.

"Waiting for me?" he asked her.

"Certainly not!"

"I think you were. You have that look about you, as if you're waiting for your lover's return. A soft, dreamy look that becomes you better than the bad temper I last saw on your face."

Gemma forced herself upright. Waiting for her lover indeed!

"Where's Gisela?" she asked with commendable *sang froid*.

His eyes snapped with amusement at her expense. "Jealous?" he suggested.

He was impossible! Worse than that, he was the most unlikeable, despicable, horrible person she had ever met! Well, she had tried to be polite, but she would try no longer. She would take a leaf out of his book and be as rude as she liked.

She turned on her heel and made for the stairs, her high heels tapping out a message of hate on the marble tiles. But he moved quickly and was at the foot of the stairs before her.

"Why won't you admit it?" he accused her. His fingers dug into her arm as he pulled her up against him. "You're jealous and spoiled! You have far too high an idea of your own importance, *piccina*. Gisela is worth more than you and your sister put together!"

"Then why don't you leave me alone?" Gemma demanded.

"I can't, and you know why. But, by God, if you don't learn soon who and what you were born to be, I shall school you in your lessons myself! It's time you learned to consider somebody other than your beautiful self."

She took a deep breath. "That's not a lesson I'm likely to learn from you! Please let me go. You're hurting me!"

"Not as much as I shall in a moment! Why won't you accept the hand life has dealt you—"

"I have! I'm an English girl, a Londoner, with an

English boy friend whom I mean to marry some day. Why won't you accept that?"

"Because you don't," he said with such decision that she blushed to the ears as she tried to deny it.

"How do you know that?" she almost pleaded with him.

He turned her round to face him and she saw the clean, rugged lines of his face lit by the golden glow of the setting sun. She thought she had never seen anything more beautiful in her whole life than he was at that moment.

"How can you deny it?" he retorted.

He held her close against his chest, lifting her onto the lowest stair to bring her head up to the same level as his. She gasped as she caught the burning glance of his eyes and felt an answering leap of her own senses. Her hands crept round the golden column of his neck without any conscious volition on her part and her mouth was open, ready for his kiss.

It was not a gentle caress. His lips were hard and punishing in their intensity and her mouth hurt when he finally released her.

"I hope you enjoyed kissing Gisela too!" she sobbed, putting a hand up to her mouth to hide it from him.

He bent his head, kissing her more gently on the cheek. "What is it to you if I did, Gemma *mia?*" he whispered in her ear. "I've come home to you now."

Chapter Eight

"Freddie, *darling,* it's so nice to have you here!"

"I knew you'd be glad to see me," Freddie answered with confidence. "You can't like being in a foreign country all by yourself. You look different somehow, Gemma."

"Grandmother bought me some new clothes."

"I daresay that's it. They don't suit you."

Freddie's face was a study as he looked at the *palazzo.* The once red and white poles looked more insecure than ever when seen through his eyes. Gemma jumped ashore onto the sagging platform in front of the door and caught her heel in one of the many cracks that grew wider every day. She took her foot out of her shoe and pulled at it madly, almost falling over as it came away suddenly in her hand.

"It's better inside," she murmured, putting her shoe back on.

"It couldn't be worse! My God, there are *hundreds* of cats!"

"They don't actually live here," Gemma informed him defensively. "They visit. Come upstairs and meet Nonna. She said she'd wait for us in her sitting room."

Freddie tripped over one of the planks of wood that covered the rapidly drying marble floor. A cloud of dust filled the air and he choked on it.

"I'm beginning to think Giulia had the right idea about this place," he grunted. "Imagine living here for longer than a few days!"

"But you haven't seen it yet!" Gemma objected. "Wait until you've seen the family portraits in the gallery and eaten your first meal in the paneled dining-hall. It's like slipping back a few centuries to when Venice was at its most magnificent."

The Contessa was dozing. Gemma wakened her by dropping a light kiss on her brow.

"Is this your young man, *cara?*"

"Yes, this is Freddie Harmon, Nonna. Freddie, my grandmother, the Contessa—"

Freddie extended his hand, his eyes glazing over as he beheld the old woman smiling up at him.

"Welcome to Venice, Mr. Harmon," her grandmother said smoothly. "I hope you enjoy your stay with us."

She rang the bell and, rather to Gemma's surprise, it actually rang somewhere in the depths downstairs and the young maid came running to see what her mistress wanted.

The Contessa looked every inch the aristocrat she

was as she directed the maid to take Freddie upstairs to his room.

"So that is Freddie," she said dryly, as the door shut behind them. "I can see why you think you like him. He is very like your father. I must admit to being relieved. If he had been a different kind of man he might very well have won you away from Marco." She shrugged her shoulders. "Your Freddie would bore you out of your mind before the honeymoon was over. Marco is never boring, is he?"

"He's obnoxious!"

Her grandmother chuckled. "Pretend as much as you want to dislike him, you don't fool me. Thank goodness it will be you who has to entertain Freddie and not me! What are you going to do with him?"

Gemma thought of the most romantic thing that anyone could do in Venice. "I shall take him in a gondola!" she said defiantly.

Freddie thought traveling by gondola to be beneath him. "They charge exorbitant rates because every tourist thinks he has to go in one at least once," he complained. "As far as I'm concerned one boat is very like another."

He put his hands in his pockets and slouched along beside her, making no effort to find a free gondola and, when Gemma had done so, making even less effort to come to terms with the gondolier, and she had to do that too, paying for it out of her own limited supply of *lire*.

Freddie stepped in first and she took her seat beside him in the elegant black boat and moved closer toward his recumbent form.

"Aren't you going to kiss me, Freddie?" she asked him.

He kissed her as a brother might have done, taking enormous care not to mess up her hair. Gemma felt nothing at all. This was terrible, she thought.

"Oh, Freddie, this isn't going to work out, is it?"

"I don't know. It takes a bit of getting used to, that's all. You've always looked so ordinary, but that dress leaves mighty little to the imagination! It wouldn't do for everyday, but it gives me a kick to think you went to so much trouble for me." He patted her gently on the arm, averting his eyes from her cleavage. "Isn't that St. Mark's Square ahead of us?" he asked.

"Yes," said Gemma.

"Good. I think I'll step ashore for a moment. It's a good thing I don't live here. I don't think I'll ever get to *like* little boats."

The gondolier helped him ashore, his grin barely concealing his contempt. "Are you going with him, *signorina?*" he asked Gemma.

Another voice broke in between them. "She's going with me!"

Gemma sat bolt upright, unable to believe her eyes. This couldn't be happening to her, but it was.

Marco grinned amiably at her. He handed over a bundle of notes to the gondolier and jumped nimbly on board, taking Freddie's seat beside Gemma as a matter of course.

"What are you doing here?" Gemma demanded.

"Helping you show Freddie Venice by moonlight as a good host should. Better still, I'll be showing it to you too! It's a gorgeous night for it, don't you think?"

"Freddie doesn't like boats," she said.

Marco was all sympathetic concern. He said to Freddie reassuringly, "The gondola does have an unusual movement, but she is a queen among boats. Come back on board and I'll show you some of the traditional features of the gondola. It will make you feel better, no?"

But Freddie preferred to stand with his feet solidly on *terra firma*. He stared moodily down into the gondola. "They're nothing more than tourist traps. Anyone can see that!"

Marco was patient. "They are older than the tourist industry, my friend."

Gemma glanced down and her eye was caught by the oar-rest as she looked up again.

"Isn't that beautiful?" she exclaimed.

Marco's enthusiasm matched her own. "The *forcola*? See how it's carved out of a solid block of walnut? No two are ever quite the same."

"Aren't you going to get in again?" Gemma asked Freddie.

"In a minute," he said with distaste. "I'd rather like to take a look at the cathedral while I'm here. You can come back for me when you've made your tour."

Gemma pressed her mouth closed, swallowing the retort that sprang to her lips. Marco took her hand in his and nodded to the gondolier to move on.

"We shouldn't have left him on his own," Gemma protested, feeling guilty because of the fierce gladness that filled her at being alone with Marco.

"You have me with you, *piccina*," Marco said in her ear. "Isn't that enough for you?"

She refused to answer, lifting her chin to show him she was still her own woman. "I wonder who first thought of making a gondola?" she said.

They were floating past the small tongue of land on which the *dogana* or customs buildings are housed, and into the Grand Canal proper. Moonlight played on the water.

"There's an old Venetian poem in the local dialect that tells the story of the first gondola," Marco told her. "It was the crescent moon which dropped out of the sky to shelter a pair of young lovers. Gondolas have been doing that ever since. There is no place in the world where three can be more of a crowd."

"The gondolier makes a third person," Gemma reminded him primly.

"He is trained to sing and not to look."

"There's nothing to see," she pointed out in prickly tones, edging away from the beguiling heat of Marco's body.

She turned her head and looked at the gondolier as he maneuvered the massive oar through the water. It was true, she thought, that he never so much as glanced at his passengers, so intent was he on his own task. And then he opened his mouth and began to sing snatches first of this opera and then of that, his voice rich and full as are so many Italian tenors. The sound carried across the water, taking on a new resonance as they passed through the high facades of the palaces which lined the Grand Canal.

Marco allowed her to move away, making no attempt to close the gap between them.

"You would think," he said, "we were passing

through the remnants of the greatest age of Venetian history, but we're not. Today, we can see virtually nothing of the period of the Republic's greatest power. Almost all these buildings are of a more recent date, the era of Venice's decline and decadence."

Gemma would have been more interested if she could have forgotten, even for a moment, the powerful physical attractions of the man seated next to her.

"Tell me about the palaces," she bade him in a husky voice.

"What do you want to know? How and why they were built?"

She nodded her head. In the dark they were far more beautiful than she had thought them in the full light of day. She could almost imagine how it had been when those ladies, who had looked so much like herself, had teetered on their ridiculous clogs up to twenty inches high, attending one elegant party after another.

"They were built as a proof of wealth, why else?" Marco interrupted her revery. "The Venetian aristocracy—and to a great extent the aristocracy was Venice—never went in for the primogeniture system of inheritance you had in England. There were no titular heads of families as such. In all Venice there are only two palaces which are still inhabited by the families who built them."

"Is Nonna's one of them?"

"I think not."

"I suppose that's why she doesn't mind your having it," Gemma consoled herself.

His face was thoughtful. "Possibly. Until the fall of the Republic there was only one palace in Venice, the

Palazzo Ducale, the others, no matter how grand they were, were merely *case*. After the fall, the patricians forgot all their republican sympathies. They all became counts of the Austrian Empire.''

Gemma felt rather let down. "Is that where Nonna's title came from?''

"Probably," Marco said cheerfully. "The history of Venice is full of such ironies. It was a republic, ruled by an aristocracy along lines which would not disgrace a modern welfare state. This aristocracy enjoyed the prestige of their ancient pedigrees, yet they didn't believe in the older son inheriting all from his father. They based the rank of their aristocracy on their success as merchants and bureaucrats, as well as their ability to keep the other states out of their business. Business might be anything from collecting local territories to buying and selling merchandise from China.''

"A strange people," Gemma agreed with a smile. "Yet you and I both sprang from their loins—''

"Not I!" he denied. "The poor were never made citizens of Venice.''

"Then you owe Venice no loyalty?'' she accused him.

"Venice has my loyalty because she has my love." He gestured across the Canal. "There is one of the Contarini Palaces, the Pallazo Contarini dei Cavalli.''

She wanted to look where he was pointing, but somehow she couldn't get past the profile of his face. She stared at him until she thought he must feel her looking at him, for his glance met hers squarely, a mute look of inquiry in his slightly raised brows.

Gemma's interest in the palaces drained away. "I don't believe your ancestors were so far removed from mine." She forced herself to say anything to break the electric silence between them before the storm burst about her ears.

"Your ancestors had different interests than mine. When, in 1299, the Republic passed laws restricting the ostentation of their citizens and, later still, decreed other laws governing what people might wear, even introducing some special magistrates to enforce the laws, it was your ancestors who were affected. Mine had no interest in the proceedings."

She eyed him doubtfully. "Don't you think you're being pompous?" she asked him. "I suppose your ancestors were above such mummery?"

"Below," he said promptly.

"And what happened to all these laws?" she demanded.

"I regret to say they were ignored by everyone concerned. Even the Patriarch of Venice tried to make the people think of higher things by fobidding the use of excessive jewelry and ornamentation, but the women appealed over his head to the Pope and won their case."

"Perhaps they had nothing else to think about," Gemma said defensively. "What did they do with their time?"

"Talked about clothes and babies—and made love."

"With their husbands?"

"Sometimes."

She hoped he wouldn't notice the heat in her face. "But your ancestors were different, I suppose?"

"They made love too," he assured her. "I like to think they made love very well!"

As he probably did. No, certainly did, she corrected herself. She knew that much about him from personal experience.

"Didn't the Venetian women do anything outside their homes?" she asked him. Perhaps he thought her home and family should be the whole sum of a woman's existence even today? She persisted, "What did the women of your family do?"

"They enjoyed the equality that poverty brings, just as the poor people of Venice do today. They worked beside their men and, in their moments of leisure, they sat in the sun on the quays beside the canals, busy with their knitting and their tongues. The sharpness of her ribald wit won my mother most arguments in our household when I was a child, and it was probably always the same."

"But Nonna isn't like that," Gemma said thoughtfully.

"She is an aristocrat, *amore*. She makes her point in other ways."

"As I do?"

His fingers intwined themselves with hers. "You have yet to find the point you want to make. When you do, you will doubtless make it with great grace and in a gentle, English way—"

"But will I win?" she pressed him.

"That will depend on whether you want to. You may prefer to leave it to others to win their small victories, while you go on to seize the prize you really want, to be at the center of a man's heart and home."

It sounded very attractive, put like that. Yet, how many women had been promised that by the men they loved and had soon found themselves with very little to show for it. She might keep the home, but would she keep the owner's heart?

"We should go home, Marco. I shouldn't be here alone with you in a gondola."

Marco's fingers touched her cheek, turning her face toward his. She could see the gleam of his eyes in the moonlight and she badly wanted to reach out her own hand and feel the way his hair grew at the nape of his neck. The moon dazzled her, or was it the light from his eyes? She reached out for him, forgetting everything but him. Her hair swung free down her back as he removed the pins one by one.

"How am I supposed to explain my appearance to Nonna?" she demanded.

"Donna Maria will understand."

That was what she was afraid of. She would understand far too well!

"I want to go home!"

Marco's arm reached round her, holding her close against him. For a long moment he examined every detail of her upturned, anxious face.

"You should have kept Freddie by your side if you didn't want to be kissed, Gemma *mia*," he said at last.

With anger and disappointment in her laggard lover Gemma turned on Marco. "Don't you ever think of anything else?" she demanded crossly. "You Italians are all the same!"

His lips touched hers in a feather-light kiss. "Look who's talking!" he mocked her. "What else do you think about when you're with me, little Gemma?"

"I think of many things."

"Tell me about them," he invited her. His lips strayed across her brow, saluting either eye and then returned to her lips. Desire, urgent and wanton, welled up within her.

"You have bronze tips to your eyelashes," she discovered aloud.

His smile taunted her. "And you look like the Daughter of the Moon herself, with your pale face and hair!"

Slowly, savoring the moment, he kissed her again, his lips warm against hers. She put her arms round his neck and pressed herself closer to him, only to find herself caught in the trap of his arms as he slowly explored her mouth with his, compelling her cooperation with a ruthlessness that secretly delighted her.

One moment his hand was flat against the small of her back, sending a shiver of excitement through her, the next he had pushed her dress from her shoulders and had released her breasts from the restriction of her clothing, finding and caressing first one nipple and then the other.

She forgot to be cautious with the man who held her so closely against him; forgot even where she was. She could not get enough of him. Her own hands thrust themselves inside his shirt, halted briefly in surprise at the roughness of the hair they discovered there, and then passed on to the smooth, hard muscles of his back.

"Now tell me you are thinking of something else!" he challenged her in triumph. "You're very beautiful, Gemma *mia.*"

"You feel so good," she whispered back.

She flexed her muscles, determined to resist the temptation to fling herself back into his arms and beg for him to kiss her again. She had to remember the other women he had held in his arms, who had clung to him as she was clinging to him now, and who had briefly amused him before he had passed on to someone else.

"And you'll marry me, won't you, Gemma?"

"No! When I marry, I mean to be the only woman in my husband's life—"

"And deny yourself the joy of being loved as you ought to be loved? My darling Gemma, how little you know about yourself if you think you will be content with anything less than what I can give you."

"It wouldn't *be* less! Why should I wait at home—"

"Because that is where I want you to be. I want to know you're there, waiting for me to come home to you. It's what you want too, in your heart of hearts, *piccina*, and it's unkind of you to pretend otherwise. Would you have a man who didn't care where you were?"

Gemma didn't know what she might have answered, nor was he in the least bit interested in any reply she made. His lips teased hers apart and his hands explored her naked flesh, arousing her to new heights of passion that had her shaking in his arms.

A part of her was scandalized that she had done nothing to stop him and now, she thought, it was too late. If he wanted to possess her there and then, that other part of her, released from the restraints of her upbringing, would welcome him, delighting in his conquest of her. She gave him back kiss for kiss, her ardor matching his. There was nothing else in the world but him. She wanted only him and she was not ashamed for him to know it.

She made a last attempt to hold onto her sanity. "Why marriage, Marco? You already have the *palazzo*."

"I want a family and sons of my own."

"And daughters?"

"If they are like their mother—"

"I can't!"

He stroked her cheek. "You'll be surprised what you can do, my Gemma. You're going to be mine sooner or later and you'll enjoy that very much, but we'll do it my way, my sweet. My wife will be the center of my home, but she will not rule my life outside the house. A man should be his own master!"

He kissed her once more, depriving her of breath. Oh yes, *yes,* she thought, that was what she wanted too. She wanted him too badly to quarrel with anything he said to her now.

He leaned up on his elbow, pulling the bodice of her dress together and smiling straight into her shadowed eyes.

"You're home, Gemma. It's time for you to get out."

"Are you coming too?" she asked him.

He shook his head. "If you don't want Donna Maria to see you, you'd better go straight to bed."

She stood on the unsteady platform, her hands clasped together. "Where are you going?" she cried out.

He laughed. It was a confident, masculine sound that made her more conscious than ever of her lips bruised from his kisses and the feel of his hands on her body.

"I'm going back for Freddie, the man you find so forgettable you would leave him to kick his heels in the cathedral all night."

"Freddie?"

No wonder he didn't believe her. She burned with humiliation that she could have so easily forgotten Freddie. She wrapped her arms about her chest and hugged herself. She was feeling better and better all the time; she was treading on air and there were stars in her eyes. Because to be kissed by Marco Andreotti made it a glorious night in any language.

Chapter Nine

One of the joys of Venice, Gemma had discovered, was to arise early and wander about the city before the morning mists had cleared, when the buildings were clothed in a pearly light that was as romantic as the famed sunsets over the canals. Few people were out and about in the very early hours. An artist might be trying to capture a particular aspect of the morning light from a bridge, or a housewife might be setting out early, determined to buy the best of the fresh vegetables available in her local quarter.

Best of all was taking one of the smaller boats that were always tied up outside the *palazzo* and which were painted in her grandmother's personal colors, and rowing herself up and down the waterways. On these occasions she would dress herself warmly in trousers and a sweater, not caring how she looked, amused by the stares of consternation she would receive from the local inhabitants.

This particular morning the city was bathed in a pink light and the distinctive smell of the canals was less offensive than usual. Gemma stepped into the boat, untied the painter, and launched herself out into the center of the canal. The peace of the morning surrounded her, completely at odds with the turmoil that was going on in her mind.

The problem of Marco had refused to go away in the night. She had only to look at him to be reduced to a state of quivering anticipation. How would she ever look him in the face again after her performance in the gondola last night? Suppose he knew how she had felt in his arms? She had no reason to suppose that he did not. He was far more experienced sexually than she. She was sure she was not the first female ever to have been bowled over by the delights of his lovemaking. It was no thanks to her virtue that she had awoken this morning still a virgin. He could have had her anytime he had wanted her; she would have raised no objection. She burned with humiliation when she remembered how she had clung to him. But would it have made any difference if she had objected? He hadn't asked her if she wanted his kisses, he had taken her acquiescence for granted. He would have kissed her however she had felt about it.

It was not *his* behavior that was a matter for her concern, but her own. Far from wanting to demonstrate her independence, she had welcomed his masterful approach, even reveling in it. That was what she was going to have to do something about.

Almost without her volition she turned up the narrowest canal she had yet been down and was astonished to find herself in the little *calle* at the back of the *palazzo*. That was where Marco had lived as a small boy, she remembered, and wondered in which one of the peeling houses his family had lived. She found some steps leading up to the little square and tied the boat up at the bottom, the thought of Marco drawing her like a magnet to the place where he had spent his childhood.

A woman dressed wholly in black, her face resembling the kernel of a walnut, was hanging out her washing on a line from outside her upstairs window. She paused in what she was doing, intrigued by the sight of a stranger down below.

"What do you want here?" she asked.

Gemma looked up and smiled. "I come from the *palazzo*," she explained.

"You came alone?" The old woman sounded scandalized and a little amused too, as though the doings of the young often amused her. "Wouldn't Marco come with you?"

Gemma experienced a sinking feeling in her middle. "I didn't tell him I was coming," she said.

"And now that you are here what are you going to do?"

Gemma shaded her eyes from the glare of the sun. She liked this old woman and she wanted to talk with her.

"Can you tell me which house was Marco's when he was a boy?" she asked her.

"It still is his house," the woman replied.

"But he lives at the *palazzo* now."

"He does, but the rest of us still live here."

"The rest of you?"

"He has more family than that grandmother of yours. His unmarried brothers and sisters still live at home."

"Oh, I see," said Gemma.

The old woman straightened her back. "If you have come to see us, *signorina,* you had better come inside. Have you had your breakfast yet?"

Gemma shook her head.

"*Bene.* You may have breakfast with me. Wait there, *signorina,* and I'll open the door for you."

The old woman disappeared from the window and shortly afterward reappeared downstairs.

"Come inside, *signorina,*" the old woman bade her. "Come into the kitchen and we shall have a nice gossip together."

"Thank you," Gemma murmured. Then, her curiosity getting the better of her politeness, she asked, "Are you Marco's mother?"

"His aunt. I am his mother's sister. I was younger than she. I live here now with her children and my own. We make a noisy household, but you will always be welcome amongst us. You may call me Zia Chiara, as everyone does, though my surname is Becchi. I am aunt to the whole district."

"Did you always live here?" Gemma asked, looking round the kitchen.

"No, not until after my sister's death. She never lived to see her son achieve his great dreams. When she lived here, there were none of the conveniences that there are now."

What conveniences? Gemma wondered. It still

lacked most of what would have been considered basic necessities back in England. There were two gas rings, but no oven, only a lot of heavy implements, saucepans, dishes for cooking pasta and others of a more general type. Baskets of eggs and fruit hung from the ceiling, together with ham, blackened by smoking.

"Un cappuccino, signorina? Un panino con burro? Un toast?"

Gemma agreed to the coffee and a piece of still warm bread covered in honey. "Won't you call me Gemma?" she asked her hostess.

Zia Chiara looked at her. "Your mother named you?"

"Both me and my sister. We both have Italian names."

"And you have the look of your grandmother and Venice. I had been told as much, but now I can see it for myself."

"I didn't know," Gemma confided, sitting down on one of the painted wooden chairs. "I always thought that all Italians were dark like my sister. I still find it odd that Venetians are mostly fair."

"But you are happy here?"

"Happier than I have ever been."

"You should have come before and visited the Contessa. She has been lonely for one of her own."

Gemma looked guilty. "I didn't think I would be welcome. Giulia came every year—"

"I remember."

Gemma flushed. "It must seem strange to you but I never felt Venetian at all before I came here. In England I was as English as everyone else. I never thought of my mother's family as having anything to do with me. English families aren't as closely knit as Italian ones."

"So Marco has told me." Zia Chiara accepted the explanation, but her disapproval was still there in her voice. "Will you stay with Donna Maria now?"

"I don't know," Gemma admitted.

Her hostess unbent a little. "There is little work to do in this house nowadays," she said with a sigh. "The latest thing that Marco has brought home for us is a washing machine, but it doesn't wash as well as soap and water and a little elbow grease. Don't tell him I said so, but I go on as I have always done, hanging out the clothes in the good fresh air, as you saw me do this morning."

"But wouldn't it make your life easier?" Gemma asked.

"I am no believer in gadgets," Zia Chiara scoffed. "It's the same with all these mechanical things like cars and carpet cleaners, they all go wrong when you need them most."

Gemma repressed a smile. "Tell me about Marco when he lived here as a child," she coaxed.

Her coffee cup was refilled. "Interested in my nephew, are you?"

"He is a great friend of my grandmother's," Gemma explained.

"What do you want to know about him? He slept upstairs in one of the bedrooms with his brothers, two, and sometimes three to a bed. There was seldom enough food for them all to be satisfied. Even pasta was beyond my sister's purse on occasion. They would eat *polenta*, as all Venetians do. Have you ever tried it?"

Gemma made a face. "I don't like it very much. I thought it was a kind of pasta."

Zia Chiara shook her head, amused. "It's made from the flour of Indian corn, which gives it that golden yellow color. It's best cut into slices and fried, and eaten with either fish or liver. Eaten on it's own, it's filling, but not very exciting."

"Do you eat it today?" Gemma asked.

"But of course we eat it! What Venetian does not? But not every day as they did then, and not on its own. Now we have a diet of meat and fruit, as much as we can eat, and it's all thanks to Marco."

"Because he moved to the *palazzo?*"

"Is that what he told you?" The amusement was back in the older woman's face.

"He doesn't talk about himself much at all," Gemma said. Perhaps she hadn't given him much opportunity. There didn't seem to be much time for talking when they were together. "I don't think he thinks it would interest me," she added hastily.

"He will tell you in his own time, *cara.* Have you finished your breakfast? Would you like to see the house now?"

"Yes, yes I would," Gemma admitted. "But not if it's any trouble. If you're not prepared for visitors—"

"Isn't it Marco's house you wish to see?"

Gemma gave up any idea of pretending otherwise. "Yes," she said.

"Then come along, *cara,* and see for yourself where Marco Andreotti was born and grew up."

The house was small. Downstairs there was the kitchen, which was relatively large and comfortable, and a stiffly furnished sitting room that was only used on formal occasions. Upstairs there were three small bedrooms, each equipped with an old-fashioned four-poster bed and as many other smaller beds as could be fit into the cramped space.

"When Marco is home, he sleeps in here," Zia Chiara said, motioning toward one of the truckle beds. "This is his."

"Was he here last night?" Gemma asked. She had waited for the sound of his footsteps on the stairs the night before and she was reasonably sure he had not slept in his room at the *palazzo*.

"Last night he had other fish to fry," Zia Chiara remarked dryly.

With Gisela? It seemed only too likely. Gemma bit her lip, trying to banish the vision of the other woman's beauty from her mind.

"I think I'd better be getting back to my grandmother," she said aloud. "You've been very kind, Zia, and I enjoyed my breakfast."

"You are welcome, child. Come and visit me whenever you like, if the Contessa permits. We are never short of food these days and you could do with some more flesh on your bones."

She went with Gemma to the top of the steps, kissing her warmly on both cheeks. "There is a quick way home you can take by passing under that little alley beside the *palazzo*. That's the way the dustmen go. *Ciao, addi'o, signorina* Gemma."

Gemma stepped into the boat and pushed herself off from the steps.

"*Addi'o*, Zia Chiara," she responded.

The short-cut that had been recommended to her was damp and dark but, in a matter of seconds, she found

herself outside the *palazzo* once again. She was tying up
the little boat to one of the posts when Freddie came
out of the front door.

"Where are you going?" she asked him, surprised to
see him.

"Out."

"I have something I want to do," he explained. "You
know, Gemma, I've been thinking. There's a terrific lot
of stuff in this ruin that you'll be able to sell one day.
There's a fortune here just rotting away, but some of
the pictures and furniture would probably fetch a
fortune if they were auctioned by a reputable firm. You
may have fallen on your feet by being the old lady's
only surviving relation."

Gemma was shocked by the thought. "I am not sure I
am the heir," she said stiffly, "I think Marco inherits,
not me."

"You could contest that in a court of law."

"But why should I? Marco has done more for her
than I ever have or am likely to do."

Freddie looked disgruntled. "If I were you, I'd make
a few inquiries about that fellow. I don't trust him."

"I don't see it as being any of our business," Gemma
said firmly. "If you're really going out, Freddie, don't
let me keep you."

She was rigid with rage as she took the stairs two at a
time on her way up to her room. *Not trust Marco
indeed!*

It was difficult not to contrast the decaying luxury,
but luxury nevertheless, of her bedroom in the *palazzo*
with one of those she had seen in the house where
Marco had been brought up.

She changed from her trousers and sweater into one

of the skirts and classical blouses her grandmother had bought for her. With Freddie gone, she decided she would spend the whole day with her grandmother.

She gave a last look at her reflection in the looking glass, pleased to notice that her new hair-do was holding up so well. That was the advantage of a simple style, she thought, and gave a final push to one of the pins that held it in place. *

From the echoing halls below came the sound of a deep masculine voice singing. Gemma's heart raced as she recognized Marco's bass tones. He was coming up the stairs. She tried not to listen, but the words rang clearly in her ears: *"Coi pensieri malinconici, Non te star a tormentar. Vien co mi, montemo in gondola, Adaremo fora in mar."*

"Don't stay and torment yourself with melancholy thoughts," she translated to herself, "come with me, we shall get into a gondola and go forth on the sea."

She went out onto the landing, half wanting to avoid him, half not. The song had a haunting melody and Marco sang it well—better than the gondolier had managed his snatches of opera the evening before. She would never go in a gondola with Marco again. Never! And what was there to panic about in that? she asked herself. Yet she was shaking with it. How much she wanted to see him again, just for an instant, just to reassure herself that his eyelashes were indeed tipped with gold. But it would be foolish to see him again before she had prepared herself. Would she ever be able to really prepare herself for him, she wondered.

She started off down the stairs hoping to hide herself in her grandmother's sitting room while she made up her mind what to do next. They came face to face at the bottom of the stairs and she cannon-balled into him before she could stop herself.

"Let me go!" she adjured him, as he caught her neatly and restored her shaky balance. "Why aren't you at work? Why aren't you still with Gisela?"

"Why, you little shrew!" he exclaimed. "Why aren't you with Freddie? Haven't you made your peace with him yet?"

"I don't have to!" she protested.

He put a hand under her chin, forcing it upward so that she could no longer avoid meeting his eyes.

"I'm very glad to hear it, but you should learn to bridle your tongue, *cara mia*, before it gets you into trouble. What's Gisela to you?"

Gemma gritted her teeth. "What is she to you?"

Marco's fingers tightened on her chin. "Is that why you went to visit Zia Chiara? To find out if I had been with Gisela last night?"

"No," she bit out. "Were you?"

"What makes you think I'll tell you where I was? You're not my keeper, Gemma Savage. If you go on like this I may change my mind and refuse to marry you after all."

"And a good thing too!" Gemma retorted. "Marriage isn't the only thing in a woman's life any longer. Haven't you heard?"

"It will be in yours!"

"You're far too arrogant," she accused him. "You could never be the center of my life—" She broke off, blushing scarlet.

"No?" he said.

"Not in a hundred years!" she insisted.

He forced her mouth up to meet his. His kiss was

hard and determined, ignoring her sob of protest. He parted her lips and pressed his tongue against hers with an intimacy that destroyed her defenses completely. She shut her eyes and clung to him. When she opened her eyes again and tried to wriggle free, Marco refused to be moved, holding her easily against him with a gentleness that was deceptive for she knew he was far stronger than she and that he had no intention of giving way to her. His body was hard and insistent against hers as his hands slipped down to her hips and he held her closer still.

"Freddie isn't the answer to your romantic dreams," he whispered in her ear. "Why don't you tell him so?"

She pushed away from him, winning a small space between them. "I suppose you would have wed Giulia in the end for the *palazzo*," she said. "If she'd lived and I had never come in her stead."

"You came in your own right, *piccina*," he assured her. "And there was never any question of my marrying your sister. She would never have done for me!"

"Would she have had any choice?" Gemma sniffed.

"Not if I'd wanted her. She couldn't forget I came out of a slum, however. Not even the *palazzo* could make her forget that."

"The *palazzo* is a slum too!" Gemma said disparagingly. "A slum with personal privacy," she added, remembering the lack of that commodity in his boyhood home.

His eyes glinted, it could have been with anger but she thought it more likely to have been with amusement.

"You've made yourself very much at home in it.

You're as much at home here as I, a true slum-dweller, am ever likely to be!"

"It's my grandmother's home," Gemma reminded him. "My family have been living here for generations, haven't they?"

"For as long as anyone else." He laughed out loud, lifting her clear off her feet in a highly enjoyable feat of strength. "But your father's family didn't live here, Gemma *mia*. Your sister always longed for her home in England, so why don't you? Do you love every stick and stone of that home as you love the *palazzo*?"

How could she say she had when she had always felt a stranger in her father's house? She remembered she had once told Marco that she was the changeling in the family. She had felt at one with the grand, decaying magnificence of this city from the first moment she had seen it, and a familiar sympathy with her grandmother she had never known with any other of her relatives.

Marco smiled at her downcast face. "It seems we're well matched after all," he said dryly, "as both of us are prepared to marry each other for the house of our dreams."

"You may be, but I never shall!" Gemma exclaimed. And much good it would do him, for she had no title to the *palazzo*, or to anything else in Venice.

He ran a finger down the center of her nose. "We'll see."

She pushed against him once again, but her hands were reluctant to lose their contact with him and it was, at best, an ineffectual movement that betrayed her weakness in the face of the challenge of his potent masculinity.

"Poor Gisela," she sighed.

Marco patted her cheek hard. "It's good to know you can be jealous, *amore mia*, but Gisela will never hurt you. Go now to your grandmother who is asking after you. You came to Venice to be with her, not to be busy about your own affairs."

"What affairs?" she demanded.

"As if you didn't know, *piccina*. I could be very angry with you for bringing Freddie here if I didn't know why you did it. Come, kiss me again, and then we must both be going."

Her body arched against his as she raised her mouth eagerly to his. His hand cradled her head, imprisoning her closely against him. The sweet ache of need within her swelled and took possession of her, taking life from the touch of his lips and the strength of his arms.

"Marco," she whispered, not knowing what more she wanted from him.

"You go to my head like wine, Gemma *mia*. Hurry away to your grandmother, my love, and try not to get into any trouble today or tomorrow."

"Why?" she asked dreamily. "Where will you be?"

"I have some things to see to, which is just as well if you want to remain a virtuous woman before your marriage."

Gemma was too proud to run all the way to her grandmother's room, but she felt like doing so. She couldn't help the way her spirits leaped whenever Marco was near, nor could she control the wanton desires that came flooding in the wake of his touch. She thought she would never understand what came over her whenever he came close to her, but there was no excusing the weakness of her defenses that made her welcome his every approach. She should have resented his arrogant treatment of her, but she *could not!* On the contrary, she seemed to delight in being forced to submit to him and there had to be some reason for that. She reminded herself of Gisela who had far more right to his interest than she, but not even her jealousy of Gisela could sting her pride into wanting to have nothing more to do with him.

If she married Marco, she would have to share him. Her heart missed a beat and she paused, her hand in mid-air as she reached up to knock on her grandmother's door. *If she married Marco?* Was she seriously considering marrying him? Well, why not? What if she did have to share him? It would be very much better than not having him at all. He had already stolen her heart and her will to be independent. She was no longer her own person, no longer free to go her own way. And that was a very frightening thought. She had no means of knowing what unhappiness she was storing up for herself in a life with a man about whom she knew so little.

Chapter Ten

*Gemma Maria Savage, vuoi prendere Marco Antonio
Francesco Andreotti qui presente per tua legittima
sposa, secondo il rito di Sua Madre Chiesa?*

Gemma stirred and muttered, *"si"* aloud.

"Gemma!"

She opened her eyes, disgruntled to hear Freddie's
voice, loud and irritated, so close by.

"I'm sorry. I think I must have dropped off."

"You were dreaming of *him*," he accused her.

"Not really. I wasn't really asleep. It was more some
kind of daydream. Marco did come into it, but—"

"If you ask me, you're in love with the fellow!"

"I'm not!"

"You've never dreamed about me," he muttered.

"You can't know that." Gemma pulled herself

together. Whatever was the matter with her was certainly exhausting. She couldn't remember when she had last fallen asleep on a sofa in broad daylight. She frowned, trying to remember what she had done to be so tired. She had slept well all night and she had done nothing at all the day before, except talk to her grandmother and dream of Marco. She hadn't seen him all day.

It suddenly occurred to Gemma that she wasn't being a very good hostess.

"I shouldn't have left you alone all day yesterday," she began to apologize. "Where did you go?"

"I had things of my own to do," he said sulkily. "But I wouldn't mind your company today—that is, if you can spare the time. I thought you might like to come out with me. Doesn't your family have an interest in the Venetian glass industry?"

Gemma nodded. "I don't think it's a very active interest nowadays, but Nonna says the whole family fortune was built on glass. In the thirteenth century Venice had a virtual monopoly in Europe. That's when the *palazzo* was first built. It's been rebuilt since then, several times, I expect. The factory is now in Murano."

"Have you seen it?" Freddie inquired.

Gemma shook her head. "I don't like Venetian glass much. It's vulgar and it's apt to be a bilious yellow color."

"But if that's where your money is going to come from, shouldn't you show some interest?"

Gemma ignored that. "You mean you want to go to Murano?" she said.

"Yes."

"Okay, then we'll go. Do you want to go now?"

"If you can spare the time from dreaming of signore Andreotti," he said testily. "Venetian glass can be very valuable, you know."

"I still don't like it," Gemma decided. "I don't think Nonna does either, because there's hardly any of it in the *palazzo*."

"Are you coming now Gemma?" Freddie asked impatiently as Gemma got up reluctantly from the sofa.

"Of course." She would be nice to him, she vowed to herself. She would be as kind and as nice as she had ever been. That way she'd feel a little less guilty about him, because she knew now that she never should have asked him to come. She had wanted to dangle him in front of Marco, to make him as jealous as she was of Gisela, and that wasn't a very admirable reason for pushing him into taking a leave from his job and flying halfway across Europe.

But she could not help being irritated again when he made a mess of getting into the boat at the Fondamenta Nuova. Had he always been so clumsy? She tried to remember and was disturbed to discover that she really couldn't remember. She wouldn't have had the same difficulty in knowing that sort of thing about Marco, she was certain of that.

"I've never been out in the lagoon before," she told her neighbor, a middle-aged woman dressed in the black of widowhood.

"Often it takes a visiting friend to take us out of our own district," the woman agreed. "What nationality is your friend?"

"We're both English."

The woman looked at her in disbelief. "I beg your pardon. I thought you were Venetian."

"My mother came from here."

"Ah, that explains it. Is your friend feeling quite well?"

Gemma turned her attention to Freddie whose face had turned a peculiar shade of green.

"Are you going to be sick?" she asked him bluntly.

"I don't think so." He swallowed, looking more miserable than ever.

"We'll be at San Michele quite soon now," Gemma assured him.

Freddie looked relieved. "If there weren't this wind it might be quite pleasant," he managed to say.

Gemma liked the breeze in her hair, but she didn't think it would do Freddie any good to tell him so.

"San Michele sounds like a melancholy sort of place," she said instead. "As far as I can see it's nothing more than Venice's cemetery." She handed the open guidebook across to Freddie. "You're allowed to stay twelve years and then your bones are tipped out onto another uninhabited island in the lagoon. Charming!"

Freddie shrugged his shoulders. "They're your people, darling."

"Yes, well, one probably doesn't mind much when one's dead," she said at once. "Are you coming ashore to have a look round?"

Freddie couldn't get ashore fast enough and, to the amusement of the rest of the passengers, he took a headlong leap off the boat, without caring if Gemma was with him or not.

"Your young man is not very romantic," the widow disapproved openly. "Is he in love with you?"

"He's just a friend," Gemma said quickly. "Nothing more!"

The woman laughed, her whole body bobbing up and down in time to her mirth. "You have a Venetian lover? Much better so! We Venetians understand these things better."

Gemma pursed up her lips. "Maybe. Excuse me, *signora,* but I must run after my friend."

"We shall see you back at the boat," the woman assured her heartily. "Don't hurry back, we'll see that it waits for you."

Gemma thanked her somewhat breathlessly and darted after Freddie who was standing some distance away, staring disapprovingly at a Franciscan friar.

"Have you ever heard of Frederick Rolfe?" he asked her doubtfully as she caught up with him.

Gemma nodded. "Baron Corvo."

"He's buried here."

But Gemma was far more interested in finding the grave of Serge Diaghilev. "I know he's here," she told Freddie. "He's somewhere in the Orthodox section if we can find it."

"I suppose he's one of your heroes?" Freddie remarked disparagingly.

"Why not?" Gemma defended herself. "Actually I want to see the grave because there was such a sensation at his funeral when Lifar jumped into the open grave."

"Never heard of him!"

"He was another dancer," Gemma said mildly. "Shall we go and look for Diaghilev?"

Freddie consented to this plan with a minimum of grace. He thought male ballet dancers were outside the pale. There had to be something wrong with them or they would have taken up a decent, manly profession. But he couldn't think of anything better to do and so, guidebook in hand, he trailed after Gemma, looking at his watch every other minute in case they missed the boat on to Murano.

His temper was hardly improved by the realization that they were the last two back to the boat. Gemma couldn't understand why he should mind so much when willing hands reached out to help her aboard amidst a flurry of laughing comments. She liked to be included as one of the local people. Freddie, it seemed, did not.

"That must be Murano now," she said a little later to her disgruntled English friend.

"More canals," he sighed.

As they were going ashore, Gemma noticed all the brick chimneys of the many foundries, and was a little put off by the number of touts who came down to the boats and tried to force the visitors into their particular tourist trap. She said something rude to a seedy looking individual who had grasped her by the arm and he dropped her like a hot potato.

"There are some advantages to speaking a little Italian," she said with satisfaction.

"It's only because you allow them to be too familiar with you," Freddie lectured her. "A little reserve would be far more becoming. I daresay your Marco thinks so too!" he added nastily.

Hurt to the quick, Gemma turned her back on him. She tried to ignore his efforts to make himself understood in a strident English addressed to anyone who would stop and listen. He wanted a boat he could row himself, but he didn't want to pay the prevailing rate that would have ensured him half-a-dozen offers to rent him a boat.

Forgetting her good intentions, Gemma looked at him in some surprise. "You want a *boat?*"

"We have to have a boat to get where we're going," he answered her.

"I hope you know what you're doing," she said. "It's easy to get lost in these canals. Why don't we hire a man to go with the boat?"

"Because I don't want anyone to know where we're going. If they guess that we're going to a glass factory, they'll only insist we go to theirs. We can't spend the whole day arguing about it."

The boat lurched dangerously as Freddie stepped into it. He sat down hastily on the center strut and moved the oars out into the water. It was quite clear that he had never rowed a boat and had little ambition for the task now.

"Shall I row?" Gemma asked patiently.

"Can you?"

"I think so. We're never going to get anywhere if you insist on going round in circles like that."

"Okay, then you do it!" he snapped.

They changed places, not without difficulty, and Gemma settled down to moving the boat in one, consistent direction, very much on her mettle to prove that she could manage a boat. Freddie sat in the stern, his shoulders hunched forward to give expression to his antipathy for their mode of transport. He seemed to know exactly where he wanted to go, however, issuing his instructions at a shout.

The canals grew more narrow and down-at-the-heel as they went further into them. Green slime grew everywhere. Crumbling buildings were crying out for attention before they slithered finally into the water at their feet.

"Are you sure this is the right place?" Gemma sought his confirmation as he ordered her over to the side beside a small wooden landing stage that was no more than the skeleton of its former self.

"Of course I'm sure. It looks as though you're right in thinking your grandmother's fortune isn't what it used to be."

"Does anyone still work here? It looks abandoned to me."

"It still employs a few men."

Gemma wondered how they managed in such a gloomy building. It was only one among a clutter of red-brick, mixed with dingy stone-work. She held the boat steady while Freddie scrambled onto the landing stage which cracked ominously as Gemma climbed up beside him. "I don't think they use this entrance anymore," she said.

"I was told to come this way," he retorted. "Stay here, and I'll go ahead and spy out the land."

He stepped round a string of grubby washing and began to shout. Gemma followed him more slowly. She wondered how long it had been since her grandmother had last come here and then her anger settled on Marco. He gave the impression that he was looking after the old lady's affairs, so why didn't he do so? To allow this place to deteriorate in this way was a disgrace!

A man came running out of the building. He bowed

several times to Freddie, apparently in recognition of his arrival.

"Welcome, *signore,* welcome. We are ready for you as you can see. Please come inside."

Freddie straightened his shoulders and flicked back his hair out of his eyes. "Hello there, Luigi." He gestured toward Gemma. "This is my fiancée, the granddaughter of the Contessa Maria Valmarano di Tiepolo, your employer."

"Signorina," Luigi acknowledged her.

Gemma had never heard her grandmother's full title and she felt quite embarrassed by it. Italy had been a Republic too long to indulge in such trappings of a former age.

"I'm Gemma Savage," she said, putting out her hand. The man scarcely looked at her.

"Signorina," he said again.

"Luigi and I have things to talk about," Freddie said preemptorily. "Why don't you take a look round the factory?"

"All right," she said. She wasn't happy about leaving him alone with Luigi, but she had no reason to insist on staying with them. Italian men preferred to do business with other men, she knew that, and she supposed Freddie was going to buy a few pieces to take back to England with him.

Inside the factory the master glass blower stood beside his furnace, his face and arms a ruddy red from the fire. He was very much more to Gemma's taste than the obsequious Luigi. She stood and watched him for a few moments in silence, impressed by the ease with which he handled the molten glass.

"Have you been doing this for long?" she asked him.

He grinned at her. "My family has been in glass as long as yours has," he answered. "Convey my greetings to your Nonna when you go back to Venice."

"How did you know I am her granddaughter?"

"You're the image of her when she was younger. How much has she told you about Murano? Has she told you all about our traditions?"

Gemma shook her head. "I know Venice was founded on the glass industry, the secrets of which were stolen from the East, but that's all. What more is there to know?"

"About Murano? Not much nowadays, but in the past we were the best that Venice had to offer. We coined our own money and paid ourselves well. We refused to allow the spies of the Republic over here, and none of us could be touched in their courts unless we were foolish enough to run off, taking our secrets with us. Then it was *finito!*" He drew the edge of his hand across his throat in a dramatic gesture.

Gemma looked about her. "Are you well paid now?"

He laughed. "I'm an old man now, as your grandmother is old also. We understand one another. When we are gone, the factory will go too. There are plenty of others to carry on the traditions of Venice, no?"

He began to show her how he worked, allowing her to weigh his long pipe in her hand, and instructing her carefully in how to raise it to her lips and blow gently down it. A small, round bubble of glass appeared at the other end. He took the pipe from her and with a quick twist, a chip, and another blow down the pipe, the shape of the new ornament could already by seen. He rolled the pipe against the bench at which he was working, placed it back in the fire, withdrew it and began to work on it again, adding a drop of glass here and another there, flourishing it in the air and blowing down his pipe again.

Then, suddenly, snap with a pair of shears and there was something between a Toby jug and a potbellied harlequin standing on the bench before her.

"*Dio mio!*" she breathed.

The glass blower grinned more broadly. "You don't like it? That shows how like your grandmother you are! You could not give one of these away to her!"

"But you must make some beautiful things?" Gemma pleaded faintly.

"For you, yes. I will make you something beautiful to decorate your wedding cake."

Gemma backed away, embarrassed.

"You will have a Venetian wedding as your grand-mother wants for you," the furnace man insisted.

Freddie and Luigi came to join her by the furnace. "We need you to sign a few papers on the Contessa's behalf," Freddie told her in businesslike tones. "Will you come and do it now?"

"What papers?" Gemma demanded.

"Nothing of much importance. There's no need to look like that, darling. Your grandmother knows all about it. She asked me to do this little job for her while we were here, that's all."

"If she wanted me to sign anything, she would have asked me," Gemma said flatly.

The glitter she recognized as greed was back in

Freddie's eyes. "We can't argue here," he growled at her. "Come outside and I'll tell you about it there."

Gemma didn't want to go with him, but she thought she owed him something still. "I won't sign," she muttered darkly.

His lips compressed into a tight line. "I think you will," he said.

Chapter Eleven

"I will not sign anything, Freddie, and you can't make me do so. I would have to have my grandmother's written authorization first."

"But haven't I explained to you until I'm sick that she asked me to do this for her."

"I still won't sign!"

"Why not?"

Gemma turned away from him. "Marco sees to all her business affairs and I'll bet he knows nothing of this. My signature isn't worth anything. Don't you see that?"

Freddie took a step toward her. "Don't you understand that I spent all yesterday setting this up and you're not going to stop me now?" he hissed.

Gemma clutched at the wooden rail to retain her

balance, but it crumbled and gave way in her hand and she pitched headlong into the water below. The green slime clung to her clothes and the dark brown water went up her nose, making her retch and fight for breath. Slowly she came up to the surface and, gasping for air, she tried to gain a foothold on some part of the landing stage.

Willing hands reached down to her as the air was filled by a flood of excited Italian. She saw that both Luigi and the master glass blower had come rushing to her aid.

"What happened?" they asked her anxiously.

She coughed and coughed again, her eyes streaming. "Do be careful!" she adjured them. "If the landing stage gives way, we'll all end up in the water!"

They hauled her up beside them, brushing the worst of the weed off her clothes and clucking over her, their fright plainly written on their faces. Only Freddie stood apart, his face white with anger.

"Now will you sign?" he demanded of her.

"No!"

She thought he might hit her, he looked so furious. The smell of the waters of the canal revolted her and she hoped she was not going to throw up. Had she swallowed any of the unsavory water? She wiped her face with her damp sleeve and left a smear of green weed across her cheek.

"Nothing you can do will make me sign!" she said proudly. "I want to have nothing more to do with you, Frederick Harmon. I wish I'd never asked you to come!"

"But you did," he reminded her. "And now you've

ruined any chance I had of getting back the money for my ticket. How did you suppose I was going to pay for it?"

Gemma frowned. "How?" she asked.

He gave her an impatient look. "How do you think? Venetian glass is valuable stuff. I only wanted a few pieces I could sell in England to cover my expenses. What's wrong with that? Only you wouldn't do your part and sign!"

"But the glass isn't mine to give you," Gemma pointed out.

"You'd have done it soon enough to please that precious Marco of yours!"

"He wouldn't have wanted to steal from a defenseless old lady!"

"He's been doing it for years!"

Gemma sniffed. The back of her throat felt raw. "I don't believe you. Marco wouldn't!"

"He's allowed this place to get into its present state."

Gemma turned her back on him. "Go away!" she said.

"I'm going!" Freddie retorted.

He scrambled down the steps of the landing stage and flung himself into the boat. One of the oars slipped out of the rowlock and the boat swung against the landing stage as he tried to retrieve it. Gemma would have fallen again if the master glass blower had not grabbed her arm and pulled her closer against the wall. By the time she had recovered her balance Freddie had the oar and was splashing away from them with more speed than skill.

The three of them stood and watched him go. He was

almost out of sight before Gemma sufficiently collected herself to call out after him.

"How am I supposed to get home?" she shouted.

Freddie didn't bother to answer.

"Where is he going?" Luigi demanded.

"I don't know," Gemma confessed. "Back to England, I hope."

The Italian shook his head at her. "But he has left without the glass the Contessa wished to have taken to the *palazzo* for her inspection. Are you going to take it instead, *signorina?*"

"No, I'm not. Will you find me some transportation though so that I can get home myself?"

"But the glass—"

"I think there was a misunderstanding over the glass."

"No, no, *signorina*. The Englishman was quite definite that the Contessa had entrusted him with collecting the glass for her. He met me yesterday in the Piazza San Marco, and we agreed he should collect it from here today. I was doubtful at first, you understand, that he was acting as official agent for your grandmother, but when he said he was bringing you with him and that you would sign the release—" He spread his hands, denying all further responsibility. "What will the Contessa say if she doesn't have the glass she wants?"

Gemma found a bit of the weed in her mouth and began to choke. "For heaven's sake, find a boat and take me home!" she moaned.

"But, *signorina*—"

Gemma found herself disliking Luigi more and more

by the minute. "Telephone my grandmother and find out what she wants done yourself!" she ordered him.

Luigi's eyes opened wide. "I? I telephone the *palazzo*? I haven't spoken to the Contessa for years!"

"You manage the glass factory, don't you?" Gemma pointed out.

"I work very hard! We have such difficulties here that you would not believe. It is not like the old days when there were many people working here. Nowadays we have only two men who are master glass blowers and no apprentices at all. The others have all gone to the other factory, but we are too old to change our ways. Signore Andreotti comes here only rarely. He comes because Giuseppe here is an old favorite of the Contessa's. If it were not for Giuseppe preferring to work here and refusing to work with a newfangled furnace, we should have been closed down long ago. It's not the way I intended ending my working days, let me tell you. I prefer to manage a flourishing business, not one which is dying on its feet."

Gemma sighed. "I'm sure you work very hard, Luigi, and that the Contessa is very pleased with your efforts."

"She never says so! We have heard nothing from her for years, only from Signore Andreotti. You would think he owned the place to hear him talk!"

"Perhaps he does," Gemma suggested.

"That's no more than the truth," Giuseppe put in, nodding his head wisely. "What would the Contessa be wanting with a place like this in her old age? The Signore probably bought it from her when he took over her other factories."

"I would have been told!" Luigi insisted.

"Maybe," Giuseppe agreed pacifically. "Maybe not. Signore Andreotti is a kind man and he might not have liked to disturb us with a change of ownership. My family has worked for the Contessa's for hundreds of years. He might have reasoned that I wouldn't want to change now, nor would I want to retire because I like having something to do every day. It's my guess he decided to leave us to go as we always have, without pressing us to make decisions we don't want to make. He is a good man, that one. He is one of us."

Luigi was horrified. "But I manage this factory. I have a right to know!"

"What do you manage?" Giuseppe jeered at him. "You pack all the glass we make and send it across to the other factory. Why should you be told anything?"

Gemma sneezed. "Never mind that now," she begged him. "Please get me home to the *palazzo!*"

Luigi smote his head with his open hand. "I shall telephone to the Contessa myself. Then we shall see who manages this factory!"

Gemma shivered. "And tell her I'm here," she said quickly. "I'm wet and I'm cold and I want to go home."

"Si, signorina."

"Come in by the fire," Giuseppe invited her. "The water in the canal is unhealthy. You could have caught anything, falling in there like that."

"I must look a sight," she murmured. "I can't go home looking like this."

Giuseppe shrugged his shoulders. "We have no clothes for you here, *signorina,* but rest content, the Contessa will come up with a solution for your problem. She is never at a loss. When she was a young girl, she was forever falling into one scrape or another. Her husband had his hands full looking after her, I can tell you."

Gemma didn't hold out much hope that her grandmother would be able to send anyone at once with clothes for her to change into. She doubted even if she would send the boat from the *palazzo* all the way to Murano to collect her. Miserably, she followed Giuseppe back into the factory. She ached all over now and the sodden mess that had once been one of her new dresses was shrinking visibly from the dunking it had received.

"I will make some coffee," Giuseppe said. "Some coffee and some hot pizza and you will feel better." He clicked his tongue sympathetically. "What a thing to happen!"

"I should never have come with Freddie," Gemma murmured. "I should have known it would end in some kind of disaster."

"Never mind," Giuseppe soothed her. "If the Contessa doesn't know what to do, Marco Andreotti will look after you. He has been like a son to the old lady all these years. He will arrange everything for you and you need not worry anymore."

He looked up as Luigi came back from the telephone in the office. It was a changed Luigi, no longer the unctuous servant of the company, but a more chastened individual altogether.

"You were right," he said bitterly to Giuseppe. "The Contessa gave us away years ago. She no longer has any interest in the factory. Nor did she send the Englishman to collect any glass for her." He eyed Gemma with grudging admiration. "She says you were right not to sign. But then she asked what you expected her to do about your being stranded here? She said she could not possibly come herself in a boat for you."

"So what am I to do?" Gemma asked him.

He gave himself a little shake. "Signore Andreotti was by her side and I spoke to him about you. He said I was to take you to the cathedral of San Donato and he will meet you there. We are to leave at once, he will be waiting for you there."

"Grazie," said Gemma with real thankfulness.

The coffee was strong and black and the pizza reeked of garlic, but she found them both surprisingly palatable. She might have been a Venetian born and bred, she thought, the way she downed their food, and drank their wine, and was even beginning to think in Italian as often as she thought in English.

"I'll bring the boat round for you," Luigi said when she had finished. "It wouldn't do to keep the signore waiting."

She got into the boat with care, afraid of falling into the stinking waters again. Giuseppe waved good-bye, his smile still cheerful and friendly. She waved back, moving her feet out of Luigi's way, and he began to row, pulling steadily away from the landing stage and down the canal.

San Donato's Cathedral is situated on a crooked canal, in a sea of glass factories. Its red-brick colonnaded apse overlooks a wide piazza. Gemma looked anxiously round for Marco, but there was no sign of him anywhere. She felt self-conscious in her still damp, still shrinking dress, and she went and stood in a secluded corner, where she could be seen, but where she was not too obvious to the passing onlookers.

The wind blew cold round the piazza. Gemma hoped that Marco would come soon. She made her way into the cathedral out of the wind after a few minutes and amused herself by reading the story of the rivalry that had once existed between San Donato and the now defunct Santo Stefano.

Gemma wandered out into the piazza again. The wind caught her damp skirts and made her gasp with cold. She felt a warm coat lowered onto her shoulders and she looked round quickly to see Marco beside her.

"Come stà, carissima?"

She could hardly believe he was there at last! *"Bene, grazie,"* she said automatically. Then, "No, I'm not! I'm not well at all! I'm wet and cold and—and I'm so glad to see you, Marco!"

His arms went round her in the most comfortable way. "My poor love, what happened to you?"

"I fell into the canal." she murmured. "And I don't think I like Freddie that much after all."

His arms tightened about her. "Then you won't see him again, *piccina*. I will see to that."

She heaved a sigh, determined to tell him the whole story. "I felt guilty about him—bringing him here, I mean, when I didn't really want to see him."

"You didn't? I thought you had an agreement to marry one day?"

"Not really. I knew he was going to ask me to marry him the day you came to London, but, when it came to it, I couldn't agree to anything. He kept on talking about moving into my father's house and the money I must have inherited from him, but there wasn't any! By the time I'd paid for everything, I was probably even in debt. I suppose I still am! So, you see, I must go back to England as quickly as possible and get back to work."

"Your grandmother will have something to say about that."

Gemma's chin jutted stubbornly. "I shall come and visit her as often as possible, but father and Giulia were my family and now there's only me left."

"Sell the house, *cara*. That'll take care of all the debts and you can stay in Venice with a clear conscience."

"And live off Nonna until I find something better?" Her eyes darkened. "I couldn't do that. I don't think she has enough for her own needs these days. That factory place was awful. I've always thought most Venetian glass to be ghastly, but—"

"It brings Venice a good income from the tourists."

"But it's *hideous!*"

"Of an unsurpassed vulgarity," he agreed calmly. "But many fortunes in Venice are still based on our glass-making, mine included."

"Yours?"

"I am not penniless now as I was in my beginnings. Did you think I was still a charity boy relying on handouts from your grandmother to survive?"

She shook her head, repressing a shiver. "You gave her something too, more than either Giulia or I did!"

"Perhaps."

He felt her shiver again and cupped her cheek against his hand. "We must get you a change of clothing and some hot food inside you. *Bene*, I shall take you to Gisela's house."

"No!"

"No?" A smile played over his lips. "You're in no position to veto anything just now, little Gemma. Make up your mind to it, *carissima*, I shall not allow you to succumb to pneumonia because you are too proud to admit it would be better for you if I were to look after you. We are going to Gisela's house, and you will be polite to her, as polite as you were when you saw us together in St. Mark's Square. You should know by this time you have no need to be jealous of any other woman."

"I am not jealous of Gisela!"

"Then there is no reason for you not to go with me to her house," he answered promptly.

"No," she agreed uncertainly. "She might not want to lend me any of her clothes," she added, not liking the mockery in his glance.

"She will be glad to lend you anything you need."

Gemma bit her lip. "How can you be sure of that? If she's fond of you—"

"Which she is!"

Gemma tore free of his restraining arm. "You're so conceited!" she stormed at him. "Don't you care about her feelings?"

"We understand one another."

"I'm sure!"

"It's you who doesn't understand," he went on patiently. "Giesela won't thank you for your concern."

"But if she's in love with you?"

"She's not!"

Gemma found that difficult to believe. "Why does she meet you—"

"Because she's my brother's widow and my business partner."

Gemma sagged against him. "I thought she was—"

"I know what you thought, my sweet. You made it only too clear. I could have slapped you when you took such pains to be nice to her at Florian's."

Gemma remembered only too clearly how angry he had been with her. "I *liked* her," she claimed. "I liked the look of her when I first saw her, and I would have liked her to be my friend when I met her with you. Only, I didn't think that would be possible. I didn't think she would want it."

"You'd better ask her when you see her this time," he replied forcefully. "We've wasted enough time already. Your teeth are chattering with cold and the sooner I have you warm and dry the better."

She went meekly with him, peeping at him through her lashes as if she had never really seen him before. What had happened to his brother? she wondered. And how could Gisela not be in love with him?

"Marco—?"

"Can you run, Gemma?"

"Of course I can run."

And run they did. Even without the handicap of high heels, Gemma would have had difficulty keeping up with him, but he answered this problem by the simple expedient of putting his arm around her and almost carrying her. All she had to do was put an occasional foot down to keep her balance. Moving that way she could feel every muscle in his body against hers and a sweet stirring of desire leaped like a flash of lightning between them.

"Pity we have to take refuge with Gisela just now," Marco murmured close to her ear. "She will be very much *de trop*."

But that Gemma refused to admit. "I am looking forward to seeing her!" she declared.

"Despite what Giulia always said about her?" Marco mocked her.

Gemma blinked. "What did she say?"

"She had no time for me or my family."

"Perhaps Giulia thought—" Gemma's voice died away as she realized the impossibility of putting into words that either of them could have thought Gisela to have been Marco's mistress.

"That wasn't her difficulty," Marco said dryly. "She was well aware who Gisela was. My brother was alive in those days. Giulia simply thought that none of us was good enough for her."

"She had no reason to think herself any better than you are," Gemma said severely.

"You think not?" His tones were even drier. "She was the granddaughter of the Contessa—"

"We're very ordinary people!"

Marco came to a sudden halt, pulling Gemma round to face him, his face stern. "You don't think Gisela is common?"

"She's beautiful!" Gemma breathed. "That's why I noticed her standing there on the bridge. She's one of the most beautiful people I've ever seen."

A glimmer of amusement shone in his eyes. "Even compared with the new, Venetian you?"

"Well, of course," Gemma insisted. "I'm glad to look a little like Nonna, and that my looks are typically Venetian, but I shall never be *beautiful*."

His fingers dug into her damp shoulders. "You little fool! *Dio*, Gemma, you're beautiful to me!" He kissed her hard on the mouth.

"Mmm," she said, "you told me that once before, but I didn't believe you. I thought you said it to every girl you met."

"But now you know better, *bellissima signorina?*"

She shook her head, suddenly shy. "Where does Gisela live?" she inquired.

"Just round the corner. She lives over the first glass factory I ever acquired. It was the start of making my dreams come true."

Gemma pushed her hands into his, smiling up at him. "Did Nonna—"

"Donna Maria had nothing to do with it. She and I are friends. It isn't fitting for a man to accept help at a woman's hands."

"She accepts your help," Gemma pointed out.

"Because I am a man. When things began to go wrong for her, I took all her affairs into my own hands. She would have lost the *palazzo* otherwise."

"We should have done it for her," Gemma said, hanging her head. "We were the only relations she had left in the world."

He wound his fingers in her hair and gave it a gentle tug. "That's past history, Gemma *mia.*"

This factory was quite different from the one she had been to earlier. Marco led the way up some steps at the side of the building and hammered on the door at the top. Gisela came immediately, opening it wide, her pleasure at seeing her brother-in-law plainly written on her face.

"I've brought Gemma to visit you," he explained in flat, unemotional tones.

Gisela saw Gemma and her eyes opened wide as she took in her damp, crumpled state. She tried hard not to laugh, but she had no control over the shout of joyous mirth that rose from her lips.

"My poor one, what has he been doing to you?" she asked. "You stink like rotting fish! Come in, come in, both of you, and tell me all about it. Straight into the shower with you, Gemma, and I'll find some clothes for you. What a smell! But never you mind, my dear, all true Venetians fall into the canals sooner or later. Now you are truly one of us!"

"I couldn't ask for anything better," said Gemma simply.

Chapter Twelve

Gamma was soaping herself for the second time in the shower when Gisela knocked on the door and announced she had brought a change of clothes. Gemma found a luxurious towel and wrapped it about herself.

"Avanti!" she called out.

"Prego," Gisela murmured as she thrust open the door. She looked Gemma over, her eyes narrowing. "That's quite a bruise you have," she said. "No wonder Marco was so concerned about you."

"It hurts less than it did," Gemma assured her.

"Maybe, but I agree with Marco that it's time this Freddie person went back to England. You can leave everything to him, *cara*. He will see to it you never have to see that young man again. You'll be much happier with Marco. He is a real man!"

Gemma made a face and began to dry her hair. "But would one woman ever be enough for him?"

Gisela looked astonished. "Surely you can't still believe that he and I—Oh, how angry you made him that day with your suspicions! But he wouldn't let me tell you the truth. He said you would have to learn to trust him and his word without any help from outsiders."

"Well, I don't trust him!"

"Hasn't he offered you marriage?"

"Yes." Gemma rubbed her hair more vigorously than ever. "But not even Nonna thinks he would be faithful to me for long. She said an Italian wife had to get used to such things, but I'm too English for that. I want to come first with my husband."

"What odd ideas you have about Italians," Gisela marveled. "And your grandmother should know better than to encourage you. You have been reading too many stories about such people as film stars and the wilder members of the aristocracy, of the so-called *dolce vita*. But do you think we all live like that? Of course not! We Italians are very family-minded, more so than you in Northern Europe! We still put our families before our personal happiness. Our marriages are the foundation stones of family life. When you understand that, you can begin to consider marriage with Marco more clearly. All his family are very Italian in their ideas you know. They would never do anything to hurt their families, not even those they have adopted into their family. Marco has done much for your grandmother these last years."

"Yes, I know, but she isn't married to him. She said

her own husband had a roving eye and I would have to learn to turn a blind eye to whatever Marco did outside the home."

"Oh la! And you believed this of Marco? It could be true if you made him unwelcome every time he approached you, but you are too much in love with him to do that, no? You will be well matched, both of you demanding much from the other. And, let me tell you something else, if Marco is ever unfaithful to you, you will never know about it. He will see to that. But ever since he saw you, he has eyes only for you, so why should you worry? Aren't you woman enough for him?"

Gemma was glad she had the towel over her head.

Gisela burst out laughing. It was a warm, earthy sound that made Gemma blush to the ears. "I think you are!" she declared emphatically, her eyes dancing with barely suppressed amusement. "Now, hurry up and dress, and I will make lunch for us."

Left alone, Gemma dressed herself in the clothes Gisela had provided. There were a pair of trousers, a turtleneck sweater, and some beautiful, hand-embroidered underwear, such as her grandmother spent her time making for herself. When she was done, she followed her nose to the kitchen and began to set the table while Gisela stirred the soup at the stove.

"Isn't Marco going to eat with us?" she asked.

"He had to go out," Gisela replied.

Gemma looked at her curiously. She found it difficult to believe that the young widow hadn't developed a *tendresse* for Marco since the death of her husband. Anyone would!

"You're being very kind," she said awkwardly.

"Why not? When you marry Marco you'll be my sister and, I hope, my dear friend."

Gemma chewed on her lower lip. "Don't you mind at all that Marco might marry me?"

"Why should I?" Gisela smiled quizzically. "Marco's brother Leonardo was the one I was in love with. When I married him, Marco became my brother. Most sisters are glad when their brothers marry and settle down."

"But there is no blood tie between you," Gemma pointed out.

"There is the family tie. I would have been sad if he had wanted to marry your sister Giulia, but only because she never would have understood him. It's different with you. You will take your marriage seriously, no? You want him to be happy more than you want to be happy yourself? That is the point, you see, if you are to be one of us, you must think as we think, and Giulia could never have done that. She chose to make friends only if she could find a good use for the selected person, not otherwise. She couldn't understand that the Venetians make friends only with people they like. How else would the Contessa have befriended Marco?"

Gemma sat down at the table. "I can't believe you're not a little bit in love with Marco yourself," she said.

Gisela laughed. "You didn't know Leonardo!" She sighed dramatically. "He was like Marco, but not the same at all. He wanted all I had to give and I gave it, readily. If I were to marry again, I should have to be as much in love. And I am not in love with Marco. And Marco too is a romantic. He has had a dream ever since he was a small boy and he has made much of his dream come true. Now he wants the bride of his dreams and he has found her!"

They had just finished eating when Marco came back. He put a possessive arm round Gemma's shoulders and examined her bruises once more.

"You are feeling better, no?" he asked her.

"Much better. Gisela has been very kind, and it's nice to be clean and not smell badly anymore!"

He looked amused. "You smell of carbolic soap." He made a play at smelling her hair which was still loose from the shower. "And shampoo. I prefer your usual brand which reminds me of wildflowers."

She was astonished that he should have noticed such a small detail about her. What had those dark eyes of his seen? The thought alarmed and excited her.

He noted her hot cheeks and his amusement increased. "Are you ready to go home, *carissima?*"

She nodded silently, quite unable to speak. It was left to Gisela to make polite conversation with her brother-in-law while Gemma struggled to pull herself together sufficiently to say something sensible, even if only to thank Gisela for her hospitality.

"Thanks for the clothes and the meal, Gisela," she managed to bring out as Marco was drawing her out through the door.

Gisela kissed her warmly. "My pleasure. Come and see me again in a few days time."

Marco went down the steps first, turning at the bottom to make sure she was close behind him.

"I'm sorry, darling, if you're in a hurry to get home, but the only boat I could find to get us there is a *sandolino*. It's a good thing you're warm and dry now because it will take us some time to get home."

Gemma didn't care what form of transportation he had found for her. It was enough for her to be alone with him for a while.

He seated her in the stern and cast off, rowing with a minimum of energy. It made Gemma feel safe and contented. Even the usual *frisson* of excitement she felt in his company had gone for the moment, to be replaced by a warm, buttery feeling that still held desire, but not the wild, exotic ecstasy that he could rouse in her at will.

"You were mean about Gisela," she said suddenly. "Why were you so reluctant to introduce her to me?"

"I thought you might treat her with dismissive snobbery as your sister had done."

Gemma looked at him. "I have nothing to be snobbish about," she said.

"No? You're the granddaughter of a Contessa and you live in a *palazzo*. Gisela's background is as poor as my own."

"You live in a *palazzo* too."

"I do now," he agreed with satisfaction. "I can afford to do so now since Leonardo and I made our fortune in producing Venetian glass using the very latest equipment. When Leonardo died, Gisela took over his share of the business. She keeps the accounts straight, things like that. Women, if they are good housekeepers, are often good at that side of business. She earns her money."

A slight smile lingered at the corners of Gemma's mouth. "And does Nonna earn hers?" she asked him.

He frowned at her. "What makes you think she is my pensioner?"

"Isn't she?"

"I bought the *palazzo* from her some years ago, but she has the right to go on living there for the rest of her life. That was written into the agreement between us."

"And what about her glass factory?"

Marco shrugged. "You saw it for yourself. It makes no money now and never will again."

"And so, what does she do for money?"

She saw, not without pleasure, that she had discomforted him. "She's an old woman, Gemma, and she befriended me when I was a boy. What would you want me to do? To cast her out of the only place she has ever known as home, without enough money to keep her in wigs, let alone food? She is too old to live alone and so I moved into the *palazzo* with her."

"I see," said Gemma. She was silent for a long moment. "I suppose you paid my fare out here too, and for my new clothes?"

"I owed her that much," he replied in a low voice.

The sound of the water running under the bottom of the boat was strangely soporific. "I like Gisela," Gemma returned to her original complaint. "You should have known I wouldn't have been unkind to her."

"You were prepared to be unkind to me. You were as prickly as a hedgehog whenever I thought I was getting close to you."

"I hadn't met anyone like you before," she excused herself. "I didn't want to be married out of hand because it suited Nonna that I should be. I thought you might just as easily have married Giulia?"

"There was no chance of that! When I was poor, I

used to dream of how life would be when I was rich. I would live in the *palazzo,* of course, and I would have many beautiful things to please me, and the most beautiful of all would be my wife. I would go up to the gallery and look at all your ancestors, especially the women—"

"Naturally!" she said dryly.

He grinned. "Jealous? They could all be portraits of you, you know."

Effectually silenced, she waited for him to go on. "What do you think of me, Gemma?" he probed, still smiling. "A peasant with no right to live in a *palazzo.* That is what your sister thought."

"Of course not!" She took the question seriously. "I like you—I think. I didn't at first."

"*Like* me?"

"Y-yes."

"Oh, Gemma *mia!* And is it liking you feel when I make love to you? When I hold you in my arms?"

"I wasn't talking about that," she protested. "I was talking about you as a person."

His eyes were bright with laughter. "And as a man?" he prompted her.

She looked away. "You're very attractive, but then you know that. I'm sure dozens of people have told you so."

He rowed in silence for a few minutes and then he said, "Not enough people have told you how attractive you are, my Gemma, but I mean to tell you often in the future. You are very beautiful and I want you for my own."

"Because Nonna wants you to marry me?"

He shook his head. "Dearly as I love your grandmother, I would not allow her to choose my wife for me."

Gemma felt on safer ground. "Why not? Both she and Gisela have lectured me on the advantages of an Italian marriage. How it cements the two families together and gives security to all the children. And especially how the wife has to sacrifice her own happiness to this ideal, and not notice when her husband prefers somebody else. I wouldn't be at all surprised to hear that she wasn't given much choice in her husband in the first place."

His eyes were warm with amusement. "What you want, my dear, is to have your cake and eat it too. You want the security of marriage, but only if there is a loophole so that you can get out of it if you should change your mind in the future. If you marry me, it will last until one or other of us dies."

"Perhaps it would be a mistake to marry. I shall keep on coming to Venice to see Nonna and we could spend time together whenever I was here."

"No, Gemma."

"Why not? Nonna wouldn't mind."

"I'd mind, and you'd mind. Donna Maria needs you and so you'll have to stay in Venice from now on. Marriage seems to be the only answer to that."

"You don't have to marry me to make me stay!" she said stiffly.

"I'm marrying you for my own peace of mind!"

"Really? And how I feel doesn't come into it, I suppose?"

He sighed. "No, it doesn't," he said at last. "I'd like to give you time to grow up, Gemma, but, if I do, I shall have to move out of the *palazzo* while you're finding out about yourself and that wouldn't suit any of us, would it? Never mind," he grinned suddenly, "you'll grow up quickly enough in my bed. You might even enjoy the process!"

She looked at him, embarrassed. "You might get tired of me," she said.

"Unlikely," he retorted. "If I haven't tired of you in all these years, why should I do so now?"

All these years? Had he been serious when he had told her about the life he had planned for himself when he had still been a poor boy, living at the wrong end of the *calle?* She had seen for herself how like the portraits of her ancestors she was, and she knew of the strong likeness, especially about the eyes and mouth, between herself and her grandmother. She had learned quite a lot more about Marco Andreotti today, one way and another. She had seen the glass factory where he had first made his fortune, and she had seen that dreadful place, which had once been her grandmother's, where a few old men were allowed to work as they pleased at Marco's expense. It was the first time she had seen him as being a kind man. Would he be kind to her?

She stirred uneasily, trying to get more comfortable in the boat. She thought of the cut-out picture of St. Mark that Marco had given her grandmother when he had made his First Communion, and her heart went out to him.

"When did you buy the *palazzo* from Nonna?" she asked him.

"As soon as I had enough money to do so. It gave me pleasure to think of a real aristocrat keeping the place going for me. Two years ago, Donna Maria had a heart attack and I was told she should no longer live alone. I asked Giulia to come and live with her, but Giulia refused point blank to leave England."

"Oh, I wish I'd known!" Gemma exclaimed. "If I'd known she was ill, I would have come myself."

Marco smiled quizzically at her. "But you weren't the Italian granddaughter?"

"No," Gemma said. "I was the changeling, remember?"

"With a Venetian face and body that could fill a man's dreams for the rest of his life!"

Gemma threw him a look of inquiry, not daring to believe he meant what he was saying. "Did you nurse Nonna yourself?" she asked him.

"There was nobody else she wanted to have near her. She doesn't make an easy invalid."

Gemma could imagine. "We owe you a great deal, don't we?" she said slowly.

"You owe me nothing!"

"Oh, Marco, of course I do! I owe you so much I ought to marry you for that alone."

He didn't pause for an instant in his rowing, but she was suddenly aware that he was not always the urbane, rich man. Sometimes another man showed through, the man who had pulled himself out of the mire of poverty, but had forgotten nothing about those days and the struggle for survival with no quarter given.

"If you marry me, Gemma, it'll be because you can't help yourself, not to pay me for services rendered. You never know what I might ask for by way of a tip!"

She saw that she had offended him. "I only meant that it wasn't very nice of us as a family to have left

Nonna's illness and all her business affairs to you. Blood is supposed to be thicker than water, but ours has been pretty thin where she's concerned. I'm sorry for that."

"Was that all you meant?" he asked her dryly.

She lost her temper. "I didn't mean that you were too far beneath us to have taken so much on yourself, though you can think that if you like! I very much admire the things you've done. And I'd be afraid to offer you a tip of any kind. Give you an inch and you'd take all of me and I don't know if I'm ready for that. I'm very English in some ways. I value my independence."

"Rubbish!"

She gave him a startled glance and was relieved to see he was smiling again with all the old mockery. "How do you know?" she demanded.

"I know you, Gemma *mia*. You've had to be independent of your family, but you don't like it. Oh, you put up a very good front, but you want *me!* You've wanted me from the first moment you saw me, just as I wanted you."

"We can't always have what we want," she said primly, alarmed by the exultant wave of joy that ran through her as he was speaking.

"If one wants a thing badly enough, one can usually acquire it in the end. What makes you so different?"

"I'm not a thing!"

"Nor even a *palazzo,* nor a glass factory—"

"You don't understand," she wailed. "It's easy for you. You've always known what you wanted, but I've always been taught to cut my coat according to my

cloth. I've always had to make do. My father preferred
Giulia, and why not? They had much more in common
than I had with either of them. Not even Freddie really
loved me for myself. Why should it be any different
with you? You may want me, but you've never once
said you *love* me. And you don't care if I love you or
not!"

He looked at her oddly. "Funny," he said, "I never
thought of that. Donna Maria said you lacked confidence in yourself, but I thought you knew how I felt all
along. *Mamma mia,* whoever said a boat was a
romantic place in which to propose to a girl couldn't
have tried it for himself."

Gemma sniffled. "Gondolas are romantic," she
observed.

He looked at her more closely. "Are you crying,
Gemma?"

"What if I am? What does it matter to you?"

"Because I can't take you in my arms and reassure
you and make things better until we get back to the
palazzo."

He sounded angry and remote again. Gemma wiped
her tears away with the back of her hand and sniffled
again. "Gisela didn't supply me with a handkerchief.
May I borrow yours please?"

He stopped rowing and handed her the silk square
from his coat. It was far too good for her to blow her
nose on and so she held it awkwardly between her
fingers, pleating it and unpleating it again.

By the time they reached the *palazzo* she was cold
again. It was partly the silence between them and being
upset because she had mishandled the whole situation

between them and he might not give her a second chance. She couldn't imagine why she hadn't accepted his offer of marriage thankfully with no questions asked. She wanted to marry him more than she had ever wanted anything in her whole life, but she had been so busy worrying about what might happen in the future, that she hadn't even begun to tell him how she really felt about him.

"Well, are you going to marry me?" he persisted.

She took a deep breath. "Yes!" She put her hand in his. "Yes, please!"

"Bravely said," he mocked her. "May I ask why?"

She found herself hauled up out of the boat and set down on her feet beside him. She hid her face against him, glad of the warmth of his body.

"I love you," she said. "And it'll please Nonna."

"And me?"

She pushed away from him, searching his face with an eager look that she couldn't quite hide. "Does it please you, Marco? Are you sure this is what you really want?"

He held her close and felt her shiver. "You're cold, *amore mia*. Come upstairs and I'll show you how pleased I am. Foolish one, how could you doubt that I loved you on sight! Do you think I kiss every girl almost before we've met?"

She dissolved into laughter. "But of course I did. And I wanted you to kiss only me!"

He put his head on one side and the look in his eyes dazzled her. "In a way, every girl I've ever kissed has been you," he told her.

"And in the future?" She put up a hand and stroked

his cheek. He had taken the time to shave while he had left her to eat lunch with Gisela. He must have been in a hurry, too, getting rid of Freddie for her and hiring a boat in which to row her home. Somehow, though, it was the little compliment he had paid her by shaving before coming back for her that appealed to her. She could almost believe that he loved her after that.

"I shall have you!" he said.

They walked up the marble stairs together, both of them making for her grandmother's sitting room.

"Donna Maria is out," Marco told her when they were halfway there.

She made no answer, but they both quickened their steps. At the top of the stairs, Marco would wait no longer. He turned her to face him, looking gravely at her.

"I love you very much, Gemma *mia*. I've loved you all my life and wanted you for my wife. Will you marry me, and love me, and be the mother of my children?"

She peeped up at him. "An Italian marriage?"

He put a hand behind her head, easing her mouth up to his. "No loopholes," he confirmed. "No loopholes for cither of us."

His kiss was as demanding and as masterful as she could have wished. She opened her mouth to his and thought, while she could think at all, that there was a great deal to be said for the Italian way of life and marriage.

"I know just how it'll be," she said. "I won't be able to call my soul my own—"

His crack of laughter interrupted her reverie. "It's your beautiful body I want to make mine."

An answering desire rose within her. "I love you, Marco *caro,*" she whispered, and clung to him as he kissed her again.

Silhouette Romance

ROMANCE THE WAY
IT USED TO BE...
AND COULD BE AGAIN

Contemporary romances for today's women

*Each month, six very special love stories will
be yours from SILHOUETTE. Look for them
wherever books are sold or order now
from the coupon below.*